THE M...
BUT THIS TIME... WILL CUSTER WIN?

Brown reined his horse to a halt and jumped off, grabbing at the rifle stuck in the scabbard. He knelt and aimed, firing at the farthest of the fleeing Sioux. He squeezed the trigger and felt the weapon kick. A moment later the Indian fell from his horse, rolled over, and didn't move.

Custer joined him then. He sat there, the borrowed binoculars up to his eyes. "Stop them all," he ordered.

The other officers climbed from their horses and spread out. They began firing as both Baily and Thompson opened fire again. Another of the Indians fell, but they had reached the edge of the river.

Brown fired rapidly, pulling the trigger quickly. Another Sioux slipped from the saddle, falling on the bank close to the water. A fourth was hit and plunged into the Little Bighorn with a splash.

Suddenly the remaining Indians whirled, charging back up the hill.

"Kill them all," ordered Custer.

Remember the Little Bighorn!

REMEMBER THE LITTLE BIGHORN!

KEVIN RANDLE & ROBERT CORNETT

CHARTER BOOKS, NEW YORK

REMEMBER THE LITTLE BIGHORN!

A Charter Book / published by arrangement with
the authors

PRINTING HISTORY
Charter edition / March 1990

ISBN: 1-55773-330-9

Charter Books are published by The Berkley Publishing Group,
200 Madison Avenue, New York, New York 10016.
The name "CHARTER" and the "C" logo
are trademarks belonging to Charter Communications, Inc.

PRINTED IN THE UNITED STATES OF AMERICA

10 9 8 7 6 5 4 3 2 1

ONE

The acrid cloud of gun smoke drifted across the battlefield like an early morning fog, obscuring the sights of Cemetery Ridge. Booming cannon sounded like thunder, but the din that had marked the high point of the attack, the roar that grew out of the Angle as the Confederate forces tried to overrun the Federal position, had faded.

On Little Round Top, the men sat quietly, staring down at the horror of the blood-soaked field. Thousands of men had died in the space of an hour, an hour and a half. Brave men had been cut down and ripped to pieces. Cowards had tried to avoid the fight but found themselves swept along, like the twigs in a flood-choked river. Individual choice was overwhelmed by the sheer power of the storm.

Robert K. Brown had watched the horror of a massed assault against a partially fortified position. Through binoculars, he had seen men torn apart. He had seen men stumble and fall, their blood soaking into the dusty grass and dried fields south of Gettysburg and on the slopes of Cemetery Ridge. He had sat there, the binoculars to his eyes, long after the battle had ended and the Rebels had retreated, because he couldn't look away.

Brown was a professional soldier who had fought in Korea and Vietnam and who had led mercenaries in Africa. A big man with a massive chest and huge arms, the signs of age were just beginning to show. He had salt and pepper hair, blue eyes, and a suntanned face. And even with his experiences, in modern battles and at the Alamo, he hadn't been ready for the slaughter that had taken place during Pickett's charge.

The others around him, friends who had traveled with him on the journey of years that had brought them to the

1

Battle of Gettysburg, were in shock. The slaughter that had gone on for three long days had numbed them all. They had seen too much during those seventy-two hours.

Brown finally lowered the binoculars and stood up. Without a word, he turned and walked slowly toward the eastern slope of Little Round Top. He sat there, in the shadows created by the setting sun, and stared into the distance. He could hear firing from the direction of Hanover and knew that George Armstrong Custer was engaging Jeb Stuart's cavalry in a skirmish that would become a footnote in history.

Jessie Thompson walked toward Brown and crouched near him, looking up into his blue eyes. She was a tall woman, five seven or eight who now had short hair, cut in the style worn by many of the men who fought at Gettysburg. Her rough-cut uniform of dark blue hid her shape, concealing the fact she was a woman. Her rounded face was dirty, crusted with the dust and powder residue of three days of fighting. Even while masquerading as a boy, she was a good-looking woman.

"You okay?" she asked.

Brown shook his head. "Christ, it was a butcher's yard. Men cut down by the dozens . . ."

She glanced to the left, at the backside of the Union lines where the doctors were working on the thousands of wounded, trying to save a few of the lives.

"It wasn't your fault."

"I know that. But how can you watch something like that and not be affected. Men dying under volley after volley. Politicians should be made to lead the attacks."

"Some of them would bask in the glory, not worried about the men dying behind them."

"Maybe so," agreed Brown, "but at least they would be out there where they could be killed or wounded with the men they have ordered into the battle."

The rest of the team, the six men and three women not counting Munday who had accompanied Brown to Gettysburg, filtered back to where he sat. All of them were quiet, ashen-faced. Witnessing the slaughter of so many humans had sickened them all. There was no jubilation among them, or in the victorious Union lines. Just a disgust with what they had been forced to do. No glory. Only death.

Madeline Munday, the woman from the far future who had met them at the Alamo and asked them to accompany her to Gettysburg, stood looking down on them. She was a big woman, nearly six feet tall, who had refused to get her long brown hair cut. She had dark brown eyes that were shiny, as if she were about to cry. Her angular face and thin features gave her a slightly masculine look.

"Let's get out of here," said Brown. He looked at his tiny force, making a quick head count. "Everyone's here."

Munday pulled at the sleeve of her uniform, revealing her wrist. Strapped to it was the only piece of modern electronic equipment they had been allowed to bring with them. A micro computer that maintained a temporal link with the mainframe in the far future. It allowed the controllers to keep track of the field teams and to retrieve them when their mission was completed. She touched the buttons in a predetermined code.

"How long?" asked Brown.

She shrugged. "Ten minutes at the most."

TWO

The retrieval signal caught her by surprise. Sarah Hampton stared at the board, a big, lighted thing hanging flat on the wall above the main console. The internal computer displayed the information on it, showing not only a written location, but also a map of the local area to include the terrain, towns and cities, and anything else that could adversely affect the attempted retrieval.

Hampton was young, having graduated from college less than a year earlier. A stocky, red-haired girl with white skin and green eyes whose build might be called athletic, she had a mind like a steel trap, and was considered trustworthy. But she was new at the job, so she had been assigned the watch with no teams in the field. A routine watch, except that now there was a team asking for retrieval.

She noted the time in the log, watched the signal to make sure that it wasn't a form of anomalous propagation, and then initiated a computer self-check program. None of the procedures eliminated the retrieval call.

Convinced that she had a real signal, and certain there were no teams in the field, she left the control room, walked through the conference room behind it, and out into the hallway that was lined with color photographs of some of the great moments in history. They ranged from the execution by crucifixion of Jesus, to the signing of the Declaration of Independence and the sinking of the *Titanic*.

She reached a bank of elevators with buffed aluminum doors, and touched the key pad next to them. A moment later the elevator arrived with a soft ding and she took it up to the ground floor. There was another hallway, this one wider and brighter than the one she'd come from, and it

4

was lined with displays from various shoots into the past. Stone tools and photographs of the human race's stooped ancestors on the plains of Africa. Hairy beasts that were more simian than human. Photos of Washington's farewell to his troops, Andrew Jackson's defense of the city of New Orleans, and, coincidentally, a picture of Lincoln giving the Gettysburg Address on November 19, 1863.

Reaching the office of the project director, she stopped, took a deep breath, and knocked lightly. She hesitated, heard nothing from inside, and opened the door. David Jackson was sitting behind his large desk, the top piled with documents, files, photos, and computer printouts. There was a computer on the left side of his desk, keyed to the mainframe stored in the bowels of the building. Floor to ceiling bookcases lined one wall. Hundreds of books purchased by travelers during a hundred different shoots. Opposite them was a huge window that looked out on a park filled with trees, bushes, and flowers. The current buzzword for it was "greenbelt."

Jackson, a tall, skinny man with huge hands and no sense of humor, sat with his feet up on his desk and his hands locked behind his head. He was staring out, into the greenbelt, watching as two birds, brightly colored things, wheeled in the air above a large tree.

As Hampton entered, Jackson glanced at her and said, "I never tire of looking out there. You know, the whole planet was once a giant greenbelt." He turned to face her, saw her expression, and asked, "You have a problem?"

"We've a retrieval call."

Jackson dropped his feet to the floor, pulled the computer keyboard toward him, typing on it quickly. He said, "We have no teams out."

"Exactly."

Jackson stood up and said, "Then we'd better go down and take a look at this."

She left the office with Jackson right behind her. They used the elevator and got off seven floors below the ground. They entered the conference room with Jackson now leading. Through the glass at the far end, he could see the control console, but stopped at the brown door long enough to check the red light above it, knowing that it was clear. Since it was out, he entered.

There were three positions for the technicians and one for the shoot supervisor. Each had a keyboard and a screen. There were buttons, switches, and one key-activated switch. Target information, shoot status and statistics, and a variety of other data were presented on the computer screens, or on the large display on the wall. To the right of it was a special window, two feet high and five feet long that looked down into the shoot chamber.

Jackson took the supervisor's chair and then turned around as Hampton slipped into her position.

"Now, what you got?"

She pointed at the main screen. "Recall transmission from 1863. Spacio coordinates place it in southern Pennsylvania, but we have no team there."

"I assume that you've run the normal diagnostic checks," he said.

"Completed," said Hampton, looking at her screen. "No indications of a time distortion, no indications of a malfunction, and no indications of anomalous propagation."

Jackson rubbed his chin as he stared up at the screen with an intensity that suggested he thought he was going to receive inspiration from it. "What are the possibilities that we're getting a recall from a team we haven't seen yet?"

Hampton shrugged and pulled her keyboard closer. She stared at the corner of the ceiling for a moment, forming her question, and then began to type. When she finished, she sat back as the screen glowed a dim amber at her, telling her that it was "processing."

A moment later the screen flashed and the answer paraded across it. "A possibility," she said, "but not likely. And, nothing like this has happened in the past."

"If it's a team we haven't sent yet," said Jackson, "sometime in the future, we'll recall them anyway and this incident can be marked closed."

Hampton shifted around so that she could face Jackson. "There is another possibility. It could be a team sent into the past that inadvertently made a change that created a new history. Wiped out the record of their departure. Now they want to come home but we don't know about them because of the change."

Jackson tugged at his ear as he thought about the possibilities. Hampton's point was well taken. But there were other possibilities as well. Some kind of trick for some unknown reason, a malfunction that hadn't been found yet, an electrical disturbance, or someone trying to penetrate their organization from the outside. Not only outside the United States, but outside their own time.

"Do we initiate a retrieval?" asked Hampton.

Jackson let his eyes fall to the floor. There were too many unpredictable elements. He turned so that he could study the big board. He didn't like anything about the situation. The retrieval looked like an authentic call, but he couldn't be sure.

"Do we retrieve?"

Jackson finally shook his head. "I can see a situation developing where we wouldn't know that we have people in the past. Therefore, we'll continue to monitor, but take no action."

THREE

"I thought you said no more than ten minutes," said Brown as the time slipped away from them.

"Shouldn't have been more than that," said Munday. She sat down on a rock, hunched forward, staring at the device strapped to her wrist. She held it inches from her eyes, as if that would help her see it better. "No more than ten." Again she touched the buttons, and again nothing happened.

Then, from the left came a voice. "Hey there! What you doing there?"

Brown stood up as a man dressed in a blue uniform appeared around an outcropping of rocks. He was a small man, dirty, his uniform ripped. One of the shoulder straps was missing, but the other showed the leaves of a major.

Brown moved to meet the man, took his halfhearted salute, and said, "My people and I are resting now that the battle is over."

"Battle over?" said the man, laughing. "Can't you hear them guns? Battle ain't over. Battle won't be over till all them Rebels are pushed back to where they came from."

"No, Major," said Brown. "For all intents and purposes, this engagement is all over."

"Well, now, Colonel, you may be right, but all the gen'rals say it tain't. They think we should prepare to give chase to them Rebels."

Brown waved a hand at the dozen people with him. "Major, a regiment is made of six, seven hundred men. What you see here is all that is left of those six hundred. I'm afraid that there isn't much that we can do."

"Well, Colonel, you ain't assigned to this here hill and you ain't even on the line. You might not have many

8

troops, but you can git on over to the headquarters and make your services available."

Brown laughed and sat down on the closest rock. "Major, I'm not the least bit concerned with your advice. You are a major. I happen to be a colonel and you'd be advised to remember who holds the rank."

"Sheet, Colonel, I'm under orders of Gen'ral Sickles, hisself, so your little birdy don't worry me. I'll jist tell the gen'ral that some fancy man colonel don't believe he needs to follow the gen'ral's lawful orders." The major grinned, saluted, and then turned, retreating along the path that he had used to get there.

As he disappeared, Brown looked back at Munday and said, "If you are ever going to get us out of here, now would be the appropriate time. Before that major comes back with an armed escort to enforce the gen'ral's orders and to lead us into the fight again."

"You don't want us to disappear in front of a dozen witnesses, do you?" she asked.

"I don't care one way or the other. I want you to get us the hell out of here."

Andy Kent, a scientist who had worked on the original Tucker Transfer in twentieth-century Texas, knelt near her. Kent was a thin man with short brown hair, a mustache that had long handlebars, and a thin face. His hair, what there was of it, was a tangle, and like the others, he was dirty after three days in the field.

He took her hand and studied the device, not knowing exactly what it was. The equipment that he, Robert Cunningham, and Mary Jo Andross had helped Dr. T.R.B. Tucker invent was archaic compared to the machines used in the far future. Even with that, he thought he might be able to figure out the problem. Do something to repair it.

"It's working," she said. She punched the buttons and pointed as a small light flashed. "See, it's working. I don't know what the problem is."

Kent lifted her arm so it was only inches from his eyes and studied the device. A thin thing, six different buttons, a small indicator light, and a wafer powerpack. There was a small, digital chronometer set at the bottom of it. He touched one of the buttons.

"Code is four one two five six six one."

Kent pushed the buttons, saw the indicator flash, but nothing happened.

"Transmission is made. They should gear up at the far end, run through the retrieval sequence, and ten minutes later we're back in the future."

Brown leaned closer and said, "I really would like it if we could get out of here now. Any minute we're going to have visitors and they're not coming for our health. It'll complicate matters enormously."

"We're doing our best, but there's nothing I can do unless they initiate at the other end."

"Christ," said Brown. "Who the hell thought of that? You should be able to initiate from this end."

"Look," snapped Munday, "up until this moment, the system worked just fine. There is no way to travel with the computer support needed to assure the proper genetic and cellular mapping to get us home. Retrieval must, therefore, be initiated at the far end, once we call for it."

"I'm not interested in all the excuses," said Brown. "I want results."

Munday started to stand, facing Brown, the anger burning through her. Kent tugged at her wrist, pulling her down. She glanced at him, her eyes on fire.

"Take it easy, Maddie."

She looked at Kent. "He's no right . . ."

"He has every right," said Kent quietly. "We've got to figure out if there is anything more we can do to get us out of here."

Cunningham came toward them then. He was shorter than Kent, and stockier. He'd let the beard he'd cultivated in twentieth-century Texas grow until it touched his chest. It was a huge, black thing that climbed his cheeks, hiding most of his face. The receding hairline made it look as if he had put all his hair-growing effort into the beard. His bright blue eyes glazed out of the black, curly mass.

"They're coming back. That major and a squad of enlisted men armed with their bayonets fixed. Probably carrying orders from Sickle."

"Maddie?" said Brown.

"There's nothing I can do about it. I keep trying to initiate the retrieval, but with no cooperation at the far end, there is nothing I can do." She looked toward Kent, as if she suspected he'd have a way to help her.

"Cunningham," said Brown. "Get everyone down here now. Maddie, you'd better think of something because we're damn near out of time."

"I'm doing everything I can."

"Get us out of here. Now!" pleaded Brown.

FOUR

Hampton watched the status board as the retrieval call came again and again. The location shifted slightly, a hundred yards to the southeast of where it had been. She turned away from it, used her keyboard, and learned nothing new about the people in the field.

Jackson had sat in the supervisor's chair for a while, watching the flashing of the retrieval call but had said nothing else about it. He closed his eyes for several minutes and when he opened them, the light was still flashing. Wishing hadn't made it go away.

Finally Jackson stood, stretching like he was very tired. "I'm going back to my office. You let me know if the status here changes in any way."

When he left, Hampton tried to figure out what he'd meant. Was he telling her that he wanted her to take action, or did he just want to know when the retrieval call faded from the screen? She sat there watching as the locale shifted and the light blinked, trying to determine just what she was supposed to do. Retrieve or not retrieve?

She used her keyboard and set up the retrieval, taking it all the way to the final steps that would require her to initiate it from the supervisor's chair. She had the key to activate it. That was SOP in case an emergency arose and there was no time to summon help. Each watch officer knew how to initiate the retrieval.

She stood up and walked around her chair and then sat down again. She opened the loose-leaf binder with the plastic-coated pages. The special instructions were written with felt tip and could be wiped away for updates. She studied that for a moment, and found there was no reason for her not to retrieve the field team.

"Jackson's wrong," she said out loud. "It has to be one of our teams. There was no way around it."

She leaned forward and opened the lockbox that held the key. She took it out, moved to the supervisor's chair, and sat down there. She inserted the key and turned it to the standby position. Then, she used the keyboard, set it all up again, and took a deep breath.

Suddenly she was bathed in sweat. The interior was cooled to seventy-two degrees, but she was hot. Sweat beaded on her forehead and dripped under her arms. She wiped her face with her hand and rubbed it on the front of her blue jumpsuit. She tugged the zipper lower, trying to cool herself.

"Okay," she said, her hand on the key. "Just do it."

Then, almost as if she were a criminal trying to find the silverware, she looked around. There was no one in the conference room to watch her. The lights in it had been turned out. There was no one in the shoot chamber and no one due in for another twelve hours. Weekends were like that.

Still she sat with her hand on the key. "Do it," she told herself. "Just do it."

And then, without a conscious thought, she turned the key. She surprised herself. Turning, she hit the button to finish the sequence and then turned on the flashing red light in the hallway outside the shoot chamber. It told everyone that the chamber was being used.

Then, as she sat back to allow the computer to take over the retrieval, she remembered that Jackson had thought it might be a trick to penetrate their operation. She picked up the handset, hit a button, and when a man answered at the other end, she said, "We need security down here now."

"On the way."

On the hallway monitor, she watched as half a dozen security guards, armed with laser rifles and wearing pistols, surrounded the hatch that led into the shoot chamber. They knew not to enter while the red light was flashing.

An instant later, the security chief came through the conference room and dropped into one of the vacant chairs. "What we got here?"

"Got a retrieval call, but we don't have the identity of the party calling. Thought it might be smart to have security here when the people arrive."

"How long?"

Hampton glanced at the computer screen and said, "Three minutes at the most."

"You know nothing about the party coming in?"

"Nothing except they were on the ground in Pennsylvania about the time of the Battle of Gettysburg."

"Size of force?"

"You know as much about them as I do."

The security man stood up and moved around to the edge of the console so that he could look out the corner of the window. The chamber suddenly began to glow gold and he said, "Here they come."

The small group stood close together as the Union major and his band of armed men descended to them. He spotted Brown and yelled down, "Colonel, you and your men wait right there."

"If there is anything you can do," said Brown, looking at Munday, "I'd suggest you do it now."

The golden glow of time travel wrapped them and Brown felt suddenly dizzy. He rocked back and forth as they began to accelerate through time. The days began to strobe like the popping of a giant flashbulb. Brown slipped to one knee and reached out as if to steady himself. He closed his eyes and then opened them as the speed picked up and the ground around him faded away.

Then, suddenly they were in a bowl-shaped room, the floors and walls made of tan plastic, looking like polished oak. At first there was only a golden light, but that faded, leaving them in semidarkness, the only light coming from the window up above them, where the control room was positioned.

Munday moved toward the hatch, but as she reached out to open it, a voice boomed down at her. "Don't move. Please identify yourself."

She turned, looking up at the window. "Madeline Munday. Who the hell did you think it was?"

"What's going on here?" asked Brown.

Munday turned. "I don't know. This isn't standard."

From above came the command, "Leave your weapons on the floor and exit one at a time."

"Colonel?" said one of the men.

"If you do not comply with my instructions, you will be returned to your former location."

"What's going on?" asked Kent.

Suddenly Munday laughed. "We were successful. So successful, they have no record of us going because there was no reason to send us. We did it."

"Great," said Brown. "And now they're going to arrest us."

The hatch began to open then and one man stuck his head in. He looked around and then over at Brown and the mercenaries with him.

"Sir, if you will follow me."

Brown looked at Munday, then Kent, and finally at Thompson, who had refused to lay down her rifle.

"There is nothing to worry about," said the man.

Then, from the control room came, "If you will follow instructions, we can get this problem resolved."

"Colonel," said Munday, "we had better do as they say. If we don't, they can initiate another shoot and we could find ourselves back in Gettysburg."

"I don't understand this," said Brown. He faced his people. "We'd better comply with their instructions." Brown laid his rifle on the floor and stepped away from it. He didn't bother to remove his pistol, hoping that the men wouldn't realize he had one concealed under his uniform blouse.

Then, one by one, they left the shoot chamber and were escorted to the elevator where they rode up to the debriefing chamber on the seventh floor. As they entered, Munday leaned close to Brown and said, "This isn't right."

"What do you mean?"

"We should have had the initial debriefing in a conference room right outside the chamber. Something has gone wrong."

FIVE

Hampton was met by Jackson in the corridor outside the debriefing chamber. His face was ashen, as if he was badly frightened. He stood there, shoulders hunched, his arms crossed, and one foot tapping the carpeted floor impatiently. He stared at her as she walked down the hall, and when she was close to him, he took a deep breath.

"Maybe you'd care to tell me just what in the hell you thought you were doing?"

She stopped and wiped the sweat from her face. Suddenly she didn't feel good. It had been a mistake to initiate the retrieval without specific instructions. Now it all seemed so clear. An hour ago, it had been so muddied.

"I thought it was what you wanted."

"What I wanted?" said Jackson, his voice rising. "What I wanted? I told you what I wanted. Watch it and see if there was any change on the board. I don't believe I said anything to suggest I wanted a retrieval."

"It's too late now," said Hampton, trying for an alibi.

"Yes," snapped Jackson. "You took care of that." He was silent for a moment and then asked, "Are you going in, or are you going to stand around out here?"

"In," she said. She opened the door and stepped through with Jackson right behind her.

As soon as Jackson was in the door, one of the women stood up and said, "Thank God, David, you're still here."

Jackson looked at the woman. Tall, slim, with long hair and wearing a uniform just as all the others did. She didn't move toward him.

"David, you remember me, don't you?"

Jackson stood flat-footed, almost afraid to move. He glanced at Hampton who had stopped moving too. He then

16

turned his attention back to the woman. "I'm afraid that I don't know you."

"Jackson," said Brown, "this joke has gone far enough. We completed our mission, and your fucking around at this end was almost disastrous for us."

"Sir," said Jackson, "I don't know who you are and I don't care for your language. I've never seen any of you before."

"What in the hell is going on here?" demanded Brown.

Munday held up a hand and said, "I want a history book. A current book."

Jackson studied her for a moment and then nodded. "Sarah, why don't you get us a history book."

"Yes, sir." She turned and left the office.

Jackson moved to the head of the table and sat down. He slowly surveyed the scene. The eleven men and women wearing uniforms from the Civil War were sitting around the table in low-backed chairs. The conference table was long and thin, made of high impact plastic. It held nothing, not even a pitcher of water or glasses for it. In one corner, on a raised platform, was a holotank that could be used if necessary. Computer feed from the mainframe controlled it. The lighting was bright but indirect and the walls looked to be made of the same material as the table. They were a light blue. There was nothing on them and no windows.

As calmly as he could, he asked, "Please tell me who you are and how you managed to tap into our temporal link?"

Munday jerked at the sleeve of her uniform and thrust out her arm. "I have the device designed for that purpose."

Jackson glanced at it but tried not to show too much interest in it. "That looks like one of ours."

"It is one. We left from here three days ago."

"Then you might want to explain why we have no record of it."

Munday shook her head and then said, "Maybe because of the change we initiated in the past."

The color, what little there had been, drained from Jackson's face. "Change? You made a change? My God, you're not supposed to change anything. Observe, record, but not change. Don't you understand what that could mean?"

Munday shook her head and, speaking to no one specifically, said, "It was the change. Because we were successful, there is no record of us going because there was no reason to send us." She fell back in her chair. "I should have thought of that. We should have been prepared for it."

Hampton returned with the history book, holding it up almost as if it were a banner. "Got it," she announced unnecessarily.

"Give it to me," said Munday, holding out a hand.

Jackson nodded and Hampton passed the book to her. She flipped it open, couldn't find what she wanted easily, and turned to the index. She ran her finger down the column, mumbled to herself, and opened the text.

At the beginning of the article was a picture, a lithograph reported to have been made by a reporter who had witnessed the whole horrible three days of fighting at Gettysburg. Munday's eyes fixed on it and stared at it, but recognized nothing about it except the lines of soldiers, their banners held high, attacking into lines of other soldiers who also held their banners high and who waited to kill them. Still, there was something terribly familiar about it and she felt her stomach grow cold.

"Well?" said Jackson, breaking the spell.

"Yes," she said, hastily reading the article. It told the whole story, from the beginnings when the two forces blundered into one another, to the final day when Pickett, commanding a combined force of fifteen thousand men charged across the open ground, trying to dislodge the Union forces on Cemetery Ridge.

Finally she passed the book to Brown and asked, "Is this the way it's supposed to be?"

Jackson slapped the table and demanded, "What do you mean the way it's supposed to be?"

"David," said Munday, "we were sent back to put history on the track it was meant to follow. Somehow, somewhere, something happened, and history got screwed up. We had to fix it. Make it right."

"NO!" shouted Jackson. "Our job is observation. Answering the unanswered questions of history. We do not make changes. The risk is much too great."

Brown pushed the book away and said, "It looks right."

"What does that mean?" asked Jackson.

"It means that the battle seems to have progressed the way it was supposed to have progressed. We eliminated the problem and put history on track."

"How do you know your history is right?" shouted Jackson. "If you start making changes, you don't know what is right and what is wrong."

"Fine," said Brown, his voice cold. "Then history is as I remember it and that makes it right."

Jackson shook his head, looking like a man who was about to cry. "Don't you people realize what you've done? Any change initiated at any place could have ramifications along the whole time line. We don't know where it might manifest itself. The slightest change could bring about catastrophic consequences."

"The problem," said Munday, "was that such a change had already been initiated. We went back to correct it, and given everything that has happened here, we were successful."

Kent pulled the history book toward him, flipping through it, checking the references to the Alamo, the first place that time travel had visited. It was a short piece, talking about the one hundred and eighty defenders killed when the Mexican Army under General Antonio Lopez de Santa Anna stormed the fort. No reference to thirty odd men who arrived on March first or who left an hour before the final assault.

"Okay, okay," said Jackson, holding up his hand. "Here's what we need to do. A complete debriefing so that we can find out what you might have done to the time line. Then, absolutely no more changes."

"What about us?" asked Brown.

"What about you?"

"We don't belong here, whenever this is. We're from the late twentieth century."

"Well you can't go back yet," said Jackson. "We reintroduce you into that time frame with your knowledge of the future and we could inadvertently make a change. You have to be conditioned before you can be returned."

"We can discuss that later," said Brown. "Right now I'd like to get out of this uniform, catch a hot shower, and then find something to eat."

"That's not the way we operate here," said Jackson. "We debrief first."

"Then have something brought up here to eat."

Jackson hesitated and said nothing.

Kent had stopped looking through the history book. It lay open in front of him. He said, "You'd better get that food up here because we have another problem." He pushed the book at Jackson.

"What?" asked Brown.

"Custer wins at the Little Bighorn."

"Oh shit!"

SIX

Jackson sat quietly for a moment and then looked at Brown. "What difference does it make that Custer won at the Little Bighorn?"

Brown shrugged but didn't say anything.

"Custer went on to become president, elected in 1880 and serving only a year and a month before he was assassinated. His vice president, Chester A. Arthur, took office then, and eliminated many of Custer's plans."

Thompson, who had been sitting quietly, listening to all that was going on, shook her head and said, "What?"

Jackson went on as if he hadn't heard the question. Suddenly he was in front of a class, lecturing on the early history of the United States. He glanced up at the ceiling and said, "Custer, elected in a brokered convention, was one of the most popular of the presidents. His victory over the Sioux and Cheyenne Indians at the Little Bighorn in late June made him one of the most popular men in the country at that time and he parlayed that into popular votes, sweeping into office easily that year."

Jackson lowered his eyes and looked at the people in the room with him. "But he had some bizarre ideas. He felt that the whole North American continent should be one large country. He wanted to annex Canada and Mexico, making them part of the single super country. The opposition to the idea came almost at once. It was vocal and then violent. Those were the policies that Arthur let quietly disappear on Custer's death."

"This is interesting," said Brown, "but I don't see the point."

"The point," said Jackson, "is that I'm giving you a history of the United States . . ."

21

"Which is incorrect," said Brown.

"How do you know?" said Jackson. "What makes your version of history the right one and my version the wrong one? How do you know which is proper?"

Brown fell back in his chair, unsure of how to answer the question. In a debate over the history of the United States, Jackson would be as convinced of the reality of the current history as Brown was of his. There was no way to prove one right and the other wrong.

Kent, however, understood the situation immediately. He said, "It is a matter of perspective. You're sitting here in the future where you can be affected by the changes we made. Where you were affected by the changes we made."

"And you weren't?" said Jackson.

"No. For two reasons," said Kent. "One, we were in 1863 and the change appeared in 1876. Therefore, we were not influenced by it."

"But you started out earlier and any change made should have affected you before you began time traveling. Or rather, your starting point was after the 1876 change and you would be affected."

"No," said Kent. "Our starting point is irrelevant. You have to remember that any change made by us won't affect us because we are the instrument of the change."

Brown sat quietly, as if thinking about what had been said. Finally he spoke. "Wouldn't the traveling into the future alter our perceptions to make them conform to the current history? Conform to what is happening here?"

Kent looked at Brown and grinned at him. Arguing about time travel and the theories around it often caused people to think in circles making their heads hurt. "Obviously not," he said, seeing that the discussion had left some of the others behind. He rocked in his chair and added, "Given the nature of my work, prior to the trips into the past, I've thought about this a great deal. Especially after I realized that Dr. Tucker had discovered a method of time travel. I realized that the great time travel paradox didn't exist. I could, in fact, travel into the past to kill my grandfather before my father was born."

"No," said Brown, shaking his head.

"Yes. It's because I'm the instrument of the change. Without me, there would be no change and therefore no problem. With me, I make the change and kill my grandfather. Now my father ceases to exist, as do all my siblings, but I have to exist or there is no change."

"Your point," said Jackson.

"My point is, that we—" he waved a hand encompassing everyone at the table—"we, as the instruments of the change, emerge from it with our original memories intact, and therefore know the course history took originally."

"Which is?" asked Jackson, bored with the discussion now.

"Custer loses at the Little Bighorn and President Garfield is assassinated in 1881."

Jackson rocked back in his chair and took a deep breath. He exhaled slowly and then said, "You know, we've spent our whole time here, being careful that we don't make any changes. Our travelers are briefed and rebriefed on how to avoid just such a situation. And now you blow in here and almost demand to go into the field to make one."

"But it's not a change to affect history except to put it back on the path it's supposed to follow," said Kent. "We need to repair the damage already done."

Jackson pushed himself away from the table and stood up. "This is something that I'll have to take under advisement. We can't just return to the past and make changes on the word of people we've never seen before. Not without researching this whole thing carefully."

"Now wait a minute," said Munday. "I worked here before the last trip. I was sent into the past to fix things that had gotten off track. Sent out on your orders to repair damage at Gettysburg. This is an extension of that mission."

"That's your story," said Jackson.

"If it's not true, tell me how I got the retrieval bracelet. Tell me how I knew who you are or how I knew Sarah. Tell me how I know so much about the operation here."

"A good intelligence network would set it all up," said Jackson.

"But what would be the point?" asked Munday.

"To gain access to our equipment and our organization so that you could go time traveling. So that you could make these changes you feel are necessary."

"But you retrieved us from 1863, with a knowledge of the future and the equipment . . ."

Brown broke in. "Have someone take a look at our weapons and our uniforms. Although modeled after those of the period, you'll find modifications that are obviously beyond the technology of 1863 America. Repeating rifles that look like the breechloaders for example."

"We'll do that," said Jackson. "But you haven't answered the question."

"But we have," said Munday. "We already had access to the equipment. If we didn't, we couldn't have gotten to 1863. Therefore, our motive is something else."

"These are wheels within wheels," said Jackson. He stepped to the door finally and then stopped. He looked back and said, "You wait here. I'll have someone come by and escort you to the traveler's quarters. I've got to make a few calls."

"Jackson," said Brown, "remember one thing. It was you who issued the orders that got us to 1863. All we want to do is repair damage done elsewhere."

"Yes," he said as he ducked out the door.

SEVEN

Jackson was true to his word. Someone did arrive to escort them to the traveler's quarters. What he hadn't told them was that the escort was going to be three armed guards. Brown laughed when they showed up. He figured that his men could take the guards before any of them could get a shot off. Too many people thought that a rifle or a pistol made you invincible. All it did was make you the first target for someone who had another plan in mind.

But rather than jumping the guards, which would accomplish nothing, Brown said, "Let's go on up and see what they have in store for us."

Thompson slipped close to him, touched his arm, and said, "Maybe we should just get out now." She nodded toward the guards who didn't seem to know what they were doing.

"Maybe," said Brown, "but there's nothing for us to do here. Let's just see how this hand's been dealt."

Kent slipped over. He wanted to say something, but didn't know what. In the back of his mind, he felt that there was something wrong with the situation. The argument about possible times and the workings of the changes was something that Jackson should have been aware of. You couldn't operate a time machine without having thought of each of the arguments, but Jackson had sat there quietly, listening to the arguments as if it were all new to him.

Munday joined him and whispered. "Traveler's quarters aren't bad. We've everything we need there from a complete research library to a big display holo for entertainment."

They moved to the hallway then, moving toward the

elevators. At the doors, Brown stopped and faced the people with him. They had broken up into small groups, Thompson with him, Kent and Munday together, Pete Baily, Bob Cunningham, and Mary Jo Andross forming a group, and the others, Meg Clark, William Summers, Lemuel Crawford, and Bob Crossman forming the last. The guards stayed back, as if afraid of them.

Brown said, "Let's just take it easy tonight. No great plots or plans. Not until we learn what's going on here."

There were murmurs of agreement. The elevator arrived and Brown entered, moving to the back. By squeezing, everyone got on and one of the guards hit the button, taking them up to the top floor.

As they reached it and the bell rang, one of the guards slipped to the center blocking the exit. "You'll be required to remain here through the night. Everything you need for comfort has been provided."

The doors opened then and the man stepped to the rear. Brown exited and saw that they were in a dayroom area. Couches, tables, a holotank, and a wall of windows that looked out onto the city that was fading in the setting sun. Lights were beginning to come on. Points of colored brightness to chase away the gloom.

As they all filtered out of the elevator, one of the guards said, "You all must remain here. There is a phone on the wall. Use it if you need anything."

With that, the guards got back into the elevator. The doors slipped shut.

The moment they were closed, there was an explosion of shouting. "Colonel, we going to put up with this?"

"Let's just get out."

"Who the hell do they think they are?"

Brown raised his hands and looked over to Munday. "Maddie," he said, "you want to fill us in?"

She moved to one of the couches, started to sit down and then realized that she still wore the dirty uniform she had been wearing for three days. "I don't know what to tell you. I figure Jackson and some of his people will be around to talk to us tomorrow. Debrief us in detail about our last mission and this problem in history we've discovered. Until then, there's not a hell of a lot we can do about anything. We'll just have to be patient."

Thompson peeled off her blouse and dropped it on the floor. She unbuttoned her lightweight blue shirt, pulling it out so that the tails were hanging free. She wiped a hand over her face, smearing some of the grime that three days in the field had left there.

"I'm going to take a shower," she announced. "Unless someone has a better idea."

Brown grinned at her and said, "Me too. The rest of you are big boys and girls. You can take care of yourselves for a while, can't you?"

Without waiting for an answer, the two of them walked down the wide, brightly lighted hall. Thompson opened a door, found a room that was reminiscent of a Holiday Inn. A large bed, a combination of dresser and desk. There was a window that looked out on the city. Thompson crossed to it and took off the dirty shirt, leaving her bare to the waist.

"What do you think of all this?" she asked.

Brown shook his head. He took off his blouse, looking for a place to hang it and then decided that it didn't matter. He tossed it on the desk. "I'm not going to worry about it now. Tomorrow, but not now." He sat down on the bed and took off his boots, dropping them on the floor.

Thompson turned and said, "I'll take my shower first."

Brown laughed. "Why?"

"Well, because . . ."

"I'm not going to argue with you about it. I'm just going to join you."

"That's fine with me." She flashed a smile at him.

Brown stood up. He took the pistol from the rear of his trousers where it had nestled in the small of his back. He looked around and then pulled down the bedspread so that he could shove it up under the pillow.

Now Thompson sat down on the bed and pulled up her pants leg. She'd tucked her pistol into the top of her boot.

"Isn't that uncomfortable?"

"Hell, it's rubbed my ankle raw but no one's likely to find it there."

"Hell, Jessie, we get searched by someone who knows

what he's doing, they're going to find the weapon no matter how well you hide it."

She shrugged and tossed it casually to the bed. "In that case, I won't bother hiding it." She took off her boots and then stood up, unfastening the button at the waist of her pants. She pushed them over her hips and let them fall to the floor. She kicked them away.

"You look good," said Brown.

"Give me a few minutes in the shower and I'll look even better."

Brown moved to the door and then noticed that there was no lock on it. Anyone could walk in at any time. He turned but there was nothing he could use to block it. He'd have to hope that the others would realize the room was occupied.

Thompson stripped off her underwear and stood there completely naked. There was dirt streaked on her hands, arms, face, and neck. The rest of her body didn't look dirty.

"You going to watch, or you going to help?"

"Help," said Brown. He peeled off his shirt and then took off his pants. "We didn't plan this shower very well because we don't have anything clean to put on."

Thompson opened the double doors, sliding them to the side. On the shelf was a thin blanket that looked as if it had been made of aluminum foil. There were wrinkled coveralls on a rack. They looked to have been made for a child, but the material stretched.

"Here's the clothes."

Brown padded to the bathroom. It was all white tile and stainless steel. "Here's something that hasn't changed in the last half century."

Thompson joined him and turned on the shower, holding out her hand to test the water. "There," she said, stepping into the fine spray.

Brown watched her for a moment and then climbed in with her. She glanced over her shoulder and asked, "Not too hot for you, is it?"

"It's fine," he said.

• • •

Kent stood at the window and watched as the last of the sunlight faded away. The city, spread out below him, was ablaze with light. Amber lights along the streets, blue lights and red lights and green lights from the center of the city, and then yellow and white lights from the houses and apartments. It was a city that somehow looked cleaner than those from his own time. Maybe it was the air. No smog hanging in it. No smoke, or exhaust fumes or diesel clouds. Clean, fresh air.

Munday stepped up behind him and put her hand on his shoulder. "Beautiful, isn't it?"

"Yeah," he said.

"The people from your era didn't pay attention to clean air. The government kept rolling back the standards at the insistence of big business . . ."

"That's not fair," said Kent automatically.

"You a champion of big business?"

"No," said Kent. "But they're not the only ones who are guilty. All the environment freaks would drive to their protest meetings, putting out their share of the particulate matter, and then complain because the government refused to enforce tough clean air standards. Our problem was that everyone figured the problem was someone else's to solve and that someone else was the guilty party."

"We don't have that problem." She laughed. "No, it's not that we are more responsible. We ran out of fossil fuels about fifty years ago and were forced to develop alternate sources of power. Solar, wind, and back to hydroelectric, but there are refinements that increased the output."

Kent glanced at her. "I'm not sure that I'm interested in talking about why your air is cleaner than ours. Or how you've developed cleaner forms of power."

"Forced into it by the waste of your time."

"Who found themselves living with the mistakes made by the generation before. We were thrilled with the development of atomic power. Bombs that could end life in a single bright flash or end it slowly in a poisoning of the environment." He looked down, at the park that surrounded the building.

"Let's go find a room and take a shower," said Munday.

Kent turned his attention to her and smiled. "Say, we've only known each other for a couple of days . . ."

"We met in 1836 and that was centuries ago. We've known each other longer than any couple."

"Time travel will do that to you."

She reached down for his hand and tugged at it. "Let's go. Find a room."

"Can we room together?" asked Kent.

"Why not? We're both adults. No one cares what we do, as long as we don't set the place on fire or break up the furniture."

Kent turned away from the window then. Baily and Crawford were sitting on a couch, watching some kind of game being played on the floor in front of them. The holo-tank formed the image on the floor so that it looked as if men and women, no more than a foot tall, were playing right in the room. It could be adjusted so that the players were in midair, hovering over the bed or near the chair.

"You can watch the game in our room, if you're that interested in it."

"Not that, but in the holograms being made."

"Whatever," she said. She started down the hall, stopped and looked back, over her shoulder. "You coming?"

Kent followed her as she walked away. She kept going, passing up several open doors. She turned into a corner room and said, "This one has the best view."

Kent wasn't sure that he cared about the view. Munday walked to the curtains and pulled them back. There was a corner window, floor to ceiling that opened on the whole of the city, showing it all the way out to the ocean, a thin, light line barely visible now that the sun was gone. There were aircraft in the sky, some of them moving slowly, so far away that they made no sound. The lights on them, green and red and white, made them look like the descriptions of flying saucers from his own time.

The whole thing looked like some science fiction writer's vision of the future. A bright city, streets that were paved with grass, clean, short buildings. No cars, but mass transit. People movers, monorail trains that were suspended from poles in much the same fashion as gondolas that took people up mountains.

He turned away from the scene and looked at Munday. She had taken off her blouse and the faded blue pants. "I'm going to take a shower."

Kent stood there for a moment, studying her. A slim, tall woman, the product of her time and her environment. An intelligent woman. A good-looking woman. He rubbed his face and then the top of his head.

"Things don't seem to have changed too much here." He waved a hand at the window. "I mean our changes in the past don't seem to have influenced your life here."

She stopped in the door of the bathroom and turned, looking out the window. "Superficially, it seems the same. The city looks like it did when we left. I've noticed a few minor changes but nothing significant."

"Such as?"

She walked back into the room and sat on the edge of the bed. She reached over and picked up her shirt, draping it around her shoulders so that she was no longer completely naked.

"When we made the shoot, the United States was divided . . ."

"That's right," said Kent. "I forgot."

"There was an evil empire in Europe, an outgrowth of the Nazi Reich started by Hitler. No power on earth could resist and each country existed at the whim of the Nazis. The whole earth was an armed camp. Now," she looked out the window. "Now, it seems that we're at peace."

"So our messing with history had a beneficial effect."

"Yes. The question we have to ask is whether this Custer thing is important enough to pursue. Maybe the world is better for the way history was changed."

Kent turned and looked back, out the window. It seemed to be peaceful enough, but there was no way of telling from the isolated environment of the building. The surface of a desert looked peaceful enough, but there was drama going on all around, if you knew where to look. The ocean could be even more deceiving.

"Do we have the right to make that decision?" he asked.

"I don't know. You seem to think we have a crusade. Everything must be put back the way it was. I ask you why? We did what we thought was right. We eliminated the major threat, not the Rebel victory at Gettysburg, but the Nazi victory in the Second World War. Maybe we should just leave it all alone now."

"No," said Kent. "We have got to put it back the way it was meant to be. We don't have the right to alter time from the norm."

"But who's to say what the norm is? You have an idea in your mind. I have an idea in mine. Now, we have a time line that is peaceful enough. It seems, from the little we've seen, that the world is a better place. Why mess with it?"

"Because we don't have the right to say that. History was meant to happen one way. We can't modify it to suit our own beliefs."

She stood up and moved toward him. The tail of her shirt came to mid thigh. She held the front closed with her left hand. She stopped next to him and looked out, onto the city.

"What I'm trying to say," she said, taking his hand, "is that the time line we have now is not one we designed for our own benefit. It's a random line that came about because of our changes. Maybe our appearance in 1863 was enough to cause it, though I doubt that. But now, maybe it's best to leave it alone."

Kent was about to say that they had entered 1863 with one mission. To put time back the way it was supposed to be. They had not tried to make any other changes, but they had interacted with the people of 1863. They had fired their weapons into charging crowds of Rebel soldiers. They had talked to the people of that time, eaten their food, moved among them, and all those acts could have changed time. A single word, a single act, might have been enough to do it.

"Can we get out of here?"

"Sure. They like to think that once the travelers are in isolation, they can't get out to roam the city. But there are a dozen ways out, if we really want to go."

"Clothes," said Kent.

Munday pointed at the closet. "We'll find adequate clothing in there. Not the latest in fashion, but adequate."

"Then let's go out. See what the city's like now. See if the people seem to be happy."

"Good," she said. "I like that." She let the shirt drop from her shoulders as she walked to the bathroom. "You going to join me?"

Kent began to unbutton his blouse. "Of course."

EIGHT

Jackson had left the debriefing room and headed straight for his office. He didn't need some unknown travelers lecturing him on the various aspects of time travel. He'd seen more reports on the topic than anyone he could name. Not just on the theoretical aspects of it, but science fiction novels that employed traveling through time as a plot device. Every ramification of time travel had been examined by someone at some time. In either fiction or in theory, someone had thought of everything.

He entered his office and dropped into his chair. He turned to look out the window, but the shadows had grown, wrapping the ground outside in darkness. Points of light bled through, but now all he could see were the shifting shapes and shadows of the greenbelt.

He reached over, placed his index finger on the keyboard of the computer and waited until his body heat alerted the machine to his presence, and then scanned his print to make sure he was an authorized user. The screen brightened quickly as the main menu came up.

He touched it and accessed the mainframe, asking for all information that it carried on the Custer Battle of June 25, 1876, including a list of men killed and wounded and what happened to the various survivors.

The computer flashed "processing," and then the information began to scroll up the screen.

Sunday, June 25, 1876. The Seventh U.S. Cavalry, under the tactical command of Lieutenant Colonel (Brevet Major General) George Armstrong Custer, broke camp early.

•   •   •

34

"What the hell is a brevet major general?" he asked out loud. Then, without an answer, he went back to studying the computer screen.

It wasn't much of a camp, the result of exhausted men, pushed almost beyond their limits, who fell to the ground to sleep when Custer halted the regiment. With the scouts out, the men grabbed what rest they could. When the scouts returned, just after five in the morning, Custer woke the regiment and told them they were about to enter the fight of their lives. "The largest Indian camp on the North American continent is ahead and I'm going to attack it," he told the assembled officers.

The regiment mounted and moved out shortly after that, headed in the direction of the Little Bighorn and the Indian village the scouts had found. Near the headwaters of Ash Creek, Custer halted for a final consultation with his officers and made plans to divide the regiment into three battalions. Before that could happen, a small band of Sioux appeared, spotting the soldiers. Custer, fearing that the element of surprise was evaporating, ordered the regiment forward at a gallop. The Indians, using a tactic that had drawn Captain William J. Fetterman into a trap ten years before, managed to stay far enough ahead of the soldiers so that they were in little danger. When it appeared that the cavalry was slowing, the warriors did the same.

The chase lasted for nearly two hours, along Ash Creek and then across the North Fork. When they reached the Medicine Tail Coluee, about three in the afternoon, the size of the Indian village was finally revealed. It contained not the two thousand warriors that Custer and all the others expected, but as many as six thousand. The Sioux and the Cheyenne, seeing a large force of soldiers in the distance, sprang into activity. A group of them rushed from the village to engage the cavalry while others rushed around, sounding the alert.

Custer didn't wait. He, with the entire Seventh Cavalry, attacked the Indians. The first group they encountered offered little resistance. There were too few of them and they were too poorly armed. They were overrun in minutes.

They had, however, slowed the attack long enough for the majority of the braves to reach their weapons and their horses. They came boiling from the east end of the village, screaming and firing. Custer's assault was halted and he was forced to retreat, toward the west. One company, the Grey Horse Troop under the command of Lieutenant A. E. Smith, formed a rear guard, giving Custer the chance to gain the high ground with the majority of the regiment intact.

With nearly six hundred men in a makeshift defensive perimeter, the Indians couldn't exploit their numeric superiority. Custer, on the other hand, could not break out of the ring. According to fellow officers, the last thing anyone wanted was to get into a running fight with the Sioux. That way the regiment could have been chopped up piecemeal, the Indians concentrating on the elements one at a time.

The battle raged through the afternoon with the Indians taking a heavy toll of soldiers, but also losing men rapidly. With the setting sun, the Indians withdrew from the field. Custer organized scouting parties of fifty to one hundred men who probed the village, attacking quickly and then retreating. Losses were light, but the psychological advantage was great. The Indians, fearing for their women and children and realizing that Custer did not discriminate between braves and noncombatants, hastily broke camp under the cover of darkness.

At dawn, it was obvious that the Indians had fled. A token force of a hundred braves had remained to hold the Army off long enough to give the others the chance to escape. The Seventh rode over them in a matter of minutes. They burned what was left of the camp, mutilated the bodies of the dead Sioux and Cheyenne, and then withdrew to a more defensible position to await the arrival of General Terry with his column from Fort Ellis.

Custer, having brought a newspaperman, Mark Kellogg of the Bismarck *Tribune* and New York *Herald*, with him, was already sending out dispatches claiming a great victory. The Indians had been found, attacked, and had fled in panic, their strength broken. Custer controlled the field and the day, and if it hadn't been the greatest of military victories, it was enough of one to reestablish him as a hero in the eyes of the East Coast public.

Excerpted from *Custer and the Great Sioux Victory*, Berkley Books, New York, London, Rome, and Saigon: 2013.

Jackson sat back then and stared at the final words on the screen. That was the history that he knew. Custer victorious and Custer in the White House. Custer with his army growing as they formed the core for an invasion of Canada. An invasion that would move from British Columbia eastward.

He stood and walked to the bookcases and saw the number of history books that had been devoted to Custer. They chronicled his life on the plains, the Civil War, and the White House. They vilified him and praised him. Everyone had an opinion and none of them agreed. He was a great man cut down before his dreams could be realized. He was a despot, killed before his nightmares could be forced on the world.

Jackson reached out and pulled down one of the older volumes. The copyright was 1963, years before Tucker had invented his transfer and that meant a history that had remained unaltered. It was protected from the change because it had been produced before the change. Kent thought that he knew it all. Jackson had volumes that could give him an exact history right up until the second time travel became possible. After that, it was a scramble to figure out which time line was the correct one because the possibilities were infinite.

He turned and stepped back to his desk. He glanced at the title and typed it onto the screen, but before he could push the enter button there was a knock on the door. He glanced up, saw it was Hampton, standing there, waiting. He waved her in.

The first thing out of her mouth was, "I'm sorry. I thought you wanted me to retrieve them."

Jackson had been going to tell her not to worry about it because the damage had already been done, but rocked back in his chair and laced his fingers behind his head.

"What did I say to give you that impression?"

"It was the way you acted. I thought there was an SOP and you didn't want to violate that, but thought a little independent action might be warranted."

"You were reading too much into what I was saying." Jackson sat up and leaned forward, his elbows on the desk. "Next time, think before you act, and ask before you think."

"Yes, sir."

"Now, come in and sit down."

Hampton did as she was told. She glanced out the window and then looked back at Jackson.

"You might have done us a favor," he said.

"How's that?"

"Now that we've had a chance to retrieve those people, it seems that we might have sent them out. They made a change and eliminated our records of them."

"Which is what I thought earlier."

"Exactly."

"So now what are we going to do?"

Jackson glanced at the screen of his computer where his request for information on the Custer book waited for him to punch the button. "I don't know yet. I want to examine the facts and then make arrangements. Until then, I think that we'd better just keep them locked away in the traveler's quarters."

"That include tomorrow?"

"That includes tomorrow. You have the team reporting for traveling duty assigned to another facility. Right now it's important that we keep these people under observation and under control. They've already told us they've made changes in the past. We certainly don't want them running around free. Not with their knowledge. Not yet, anyway."

Hampton stood up and brushed her hands over the front of her thighs as if dusting herself off. "I'll make sure the guards stay alert tonight."

"And tomorrow we'll debrief them at length. Find out everything we can," said Jackson, "so we'll have the information we need."

"So what will we do?"

Jackson shrugged. "Probably the best move would be to return them to their own time and forget about them. Tell them to be careful with their knowledge and just send them back to 1863, where they belong."

NINE

When they finished bathing, they toweled each other dry and then walked back into the bedroom. Kent stood facing the window again, staring out into the night. Now the sun was gone, and the sky was black, but the ground was bright with light from the buildings and streets and signs. There were flashing lights of blue and red and green. Spotlights and searchlights. The city was as bright as it would be at noon.

Munday opened the closet and drew out the stretch jumpsuits. She pointed at the dresser and said, "There should be some underwear, if you want it."

Kent turned, looked at the dresser, and then moved to it. He opened the drawer, found some jockey shorts in bright colors, found some boxer shorts, and some mesh things that looked more like scrap cloth. There were some socks, T-shirts, and undershirts.

Munday opened the other drawer and took out a flimsy scrap of material and said, "Travelers aren't supposed to use their own clothes or equipment. The theory is that you wear these things until costuming provides the proper clothing. You never know what's going to be noticed by the locals."

She put on a pair of bikini panties that hardly covered anything.

Kent stood up, a hand on his chin, and studied her. "I like those. You can see right through them."

She grinned and then picked up one of the jumpsuits. It didn't look big enough to fit her, but she put it on easily. It fit her perfectly.

Kent then dressed, finding the jumpsuit to be comfortable. It had velcro fasteners on the front. It didn't exactly mold itself to his body, but fit closely. If he'd had a pot-belly, he wouldn't have looked good.

There were shoes, rubber things with a stiff sole. Once they had slipped them on, they were ready to go.

Munday sat down on the bed then and said, "Now it's going to get a little sticky. We can't use the elevator be-cause the guards will be looking for that. What we've got to do is use the stairs, take them down to the first base-ment, and then walk the length of the building and up the access steps that will lead us to the delivery docks. Open the doors and we're out."

"This a good idea?"

"Hell, Andy, we want to take a look around, don't we? You want to see what the future holds, don't you?"

"As a scientist, how could I refuse?"

She looked at him for a moment, thinking it was a strange thing for him to say, and then remembered that Tucker's three assistants had ended up at the Alamo by accident. It had been a question of being in the wrong place at the wrong time. He was a scientist first. She would have to remember that.

"Sure," she said, standing. "A scientist couldn't resist the chance to see the future."

He touched the holotank, a flat black tube about three feet in diameter, three feet long, and with a glass lens on one end. It was set in the corner and there was an area on the floor that was flat black, looking like a screen.

"As a scientist, I'm interested in this too."

"That, we can look at later."

"Then lead on," said Kent.

They did just what she had said they would. Down the hall to the stairs. Then walked down them, reached the ground floor, and then continued down one more flight. Munday opened the door slowly, peeked out, and then said, "It's empty."

Together they hurried along the hall. Kent tried to see the pictures that lined the walls, but she wouldn't give him the chance, urging him to hurry before someone saw them. They reached the opposite door and she opened it. As they entered the stairwell, she took a final look into the hallway.

No one was chasing them, no one had seen them, and no one knew that they had gotten off the upper floor.

Kent climbed the steps and stopped at the door. Munday caught him and said, "Just push on it. It'll open."

"Won't it lock when it closes?"

"So what? They'll want us back in so they'll let us in. What they don't want is us getting out."

Kent shrugged and pushed on the door. It opened into a dim garage. There was only a little light, coming from the marked exits and the huge doors that would allow vehicles to enter. One of them sat in the corner. It resembled a truck. It was long and tall, seemed to have a tractor and a trailer, but there were no wheels, no exhaust pipes, and no real place for the engine.

"Top's covered with photoelectric cells to generate power," she told him. "Storage batteries will keep it moving for several days, if there is no sun."

"I'd like to look at that."

"Later," she said.

They hurried across the garage floor that was as clean as a basketball court. No oil leaks had stained it and no rubber tires had marked it. They reached the doors and slipped along them, coming to the end where there was a single door for people.

"You ready?" she asked.

"Of course."

She pushed open the door and Kent expected alarms to sound, but that didn't happen. Instead a wall of warm, moist air hit him. It smelled strange, not of the sea or fish, but of something else. Maybe electricity, if electricity had an odor. He stepped out into the night and found it difficult to breathe, almost as if he had run a mile as hard and as fast as he could. He took a single step and felt his head spin.

"What?"

"The air," he said, thinking at first that he wasn't used to air that wasn't polluted. People born after 1950 had grown up in a world where the air was thick with particulate matter and where people with lung problems had to stay inside sometimes or risk death.

But then he remembered the air of the Alamo and Gettysburg. That hadn't bothered him. He had moved from the plains of Texas where the worst pollution had been the horse manure stinking.

Munday turned and came back to him. "Are you all right?"

He sat down on the step and closed his eyes. Sweat beaded on his face and then dripped. He was aware of it and of the air. Thick air.

"It's scrubbed," said Munday. "We have filtration plants that suck in the air, clean it, and then blow it back out."

Kent stood up and inhaled. He coughed once and then stopped. He exhaled and said, "Let's go."

"You sure?"

"Of course."

"Okay, then. Follow me." She started down the sidewalk.

Kent caught up to her and then glanced down. The sidewalk wasn't made of concrete. The material was soft, almost like rubber, but not quite as yielding. He said nothing about it.

They reached the town. Amber light everywhere. People everywhere. But not the noise of a modern city. The street was lawn and the sidewalks made of the same soft material he'd seen earlier. It deadened the sound. In Kent's time, the center of the city would be five, ten degrees warmer than the surrounding country. But with all the vegetation, they didn't have a similar problem.

Munday grabbed his hand and said, "Come on."

They moved out, into the center of things. People seemed to be having a good time. Kent could see no evidence that there were homeless or drunks or poor. There were no alleys and no trash in the streets. Music came from some places, but it was quiet music and not the driving rock and roll that would have blared from bars in his own time.

They came to a wall that looked to have been crafted from a rough, golden stone. They sat down so that Kent could catch his breath. The sweat had dried and he no longer noticed the odor of the air. He was still breathing rapidly, as if there wasn't quite enough oxygen available. Munday seemed to have no trouble breathing the air.

"What are all these people doing out?" asked Kent.

"What do you mean?"

"In my home time, the people on the street would be looking for companionship and entertainment. They'd be relaxing after a day at work but not wandering the streets."

Munday shrugged. "They are just out, watching the world. It's too nice a night to be cooped up in a cramped, hot apartment."

"Or a house?"

"Single family dwellings have been abolished. Too much wasted space."

Kent nodded. People had surrendered rights in his time for the good of all. Or rather, some had while others fought to keep as many rights as possible.

"Let's look around," said Kent.

Munday stood up and started down the street, Kent by her side. He had thought they would look out of place in the jumpsuits, but that wasn't the case. Many people were dressed the same way though many of them had modified the standard issue to his or her own tastes. Some had created shorts, others had hacked off the arms, or ripped out the backs, or sewn bits of cloth to the suit. Some people wore a togalike garment that came to the knees. A few of the younger people, teenagers, wore nothing at all. They walked through the crowd and no one seemed to notice the nudity.

They walked through the city toward the ocean. They reached a canal, the sides lined with the same golden stone that was used on the wall and in many of the buildings. The water was clear so that they could see fish swimming in it and the plants growing on the bottom. There were children jumping off the side opposite them and paddling around, to climb up steps so that they could take another jump.

An adult was watching, sitting on the wall near them. Two others stood talking behind, paying only a little attention to the children. One of the boys, about twelve, dived in, skimmed the bottom, and then stopped, almost as if he had run into an invisible barrier. He turned right and left and then tried to swim toward the surface, but didn't move. There was a burst of bubbles, as he let out some of his air. He doubled over and grabbed at his foot.

Kent took a step forward, to the edge of the canal where he could see better. Munday put a hand on his arm. He glanced at her and then at the man across the way. He didn't seem concerned that the boy might be in trouble.

Kent said, "Isn't he going to do something?"

"It's not our business."

Now the boy was thrashing around, obviously trapped. The other children ignored him. The man sat stiffly. The two other adults seemed unaware.

Kent shook her hand from his arm and stepped forward. He crouched, ready to dive.

"NO!"

Kent looked at her and the boy in the water. He had stirred up a cloud of silt. He was kicking wildly. One hand reached the surface and splashed. Still no one seemed interested.

Now Kent dived, stretching out, as if trying to pull himself into the water. He reached the trapped youngster quickly and felt the boy's hands grabbing at him. He slipped along the boy's body and reached the trapped ankle. Grabbing a handful of the tough weed, he tugged but it didn't come loose. The boy kicked, but the movements were slower, gentler, as if the life were seeping out of him.

Kent felt his lungs burning already. He wanted to surface, gulp air, but knew there was no time to do that and return. The boy had been underwater too long. Now he grabbed at the weeds one at a time, pulling at them. One came free and then another. But now the boy was no longer moving. He was floating, his hands drifting upward, upward, toward the surface which wasn't more than a foot away.

Kent yanked at the plants, grabbing them low, near the muddy bottom. Then suddenly the last came free as the curtain of black was beginning to descend, covering his eyes. He grabbed the boy and launched himself to the surface. He burst through it, his mouth wide open. He breathed rapidly, sucking in the air and trying to hold the limp boy's head above the water's surface. Still no one moved to help. No one cared enough to try to help him save the boy.

Kent worked his way to the steps and pushed the boy up, out of the water. He felt for a pulse but found none. The lips were blue and when he pulled back one of the eyelids, the eyes were bloodshot.

He knew that sometimes drowning victims could be revived, if there were people around who knew CPR and there was medical assistance handy. People, children, had survived being underwater for an hour or more. But there was no help here and the boy was already dead anyway. Even with the boy lying on the steps, everyone ignored the situation.

There was nothing more for Kent to do. The adult sitting on the wall had watched and the two talking had looked over. The children had stopped their game and lined the edge of the canal, but no one moved toward him or the dead boy.

Kent turned and looked at Munday. She stood on the wall opposite him, looking as if she was angry with him. He slipped back into the water and swam over to her. He reached up and hauled himself out of the canal.

"Why?" he asked.

"Because there are so many people that no one cares anymore. It is simpler, better, to let nature take her course than to interfere."

"Christ," said Kent. "What's happened to you people?"

TEN

It had been a rough night. Kent had suddenly decided that he wanted to see no more of life in the future. Munday had tried to explain to him that all interference was viewed as bad form. Nature had her rules and the people no longer ignored them. Besides, anyone who rescued another human was suddenly responsible for that person. The rescuer found himself accused of a crime, right along with the criminal, if the rescuer had saved the criminal's life at some time. The rescuer was responsible for the victim's debts and for the victim's medical bills and for the victim's life.

Kent argued with the concept as they returned to the building, but Munday kept telling him it was the way things were. Kent didn't look down on the way primitive humans treated their fellows.

"But you're not primitive," argued Kent.

"No, but we're overcrowded, underfed, with five people wanting everything. Good jobs are scarce. A thousand people, ten thousand, might apply for a single position. Waiting lines are hundreds long for everything."

Kent had stopped walking and looked at the people on the streets and understood. Apartments were rented by the hour. A single apartment might hold three families, and each family had the right to a specific block of time. When their time was up, they had to vacate so the next family could get in to wash and sleep. It was the concept of time-sharing taken to its ultimate extreme.

The glitz had come off paradise. They might have solved some of the problems, but there were new ones facing them. Kent wanted nothing to do with it.

At the building where they had started, he stopped,

waiting for Munday to get them back in. She had been right, the guards didn't stop them. But he noticed a ring of people forming outside. The guards were keeping them out.

"They're waiting for the garage door to open. People are allowed to use the shelter during the night."

Kent ignored her, walking to the elevator. He had seen more than enough. Munday followed him and as they waited, she said, "Don't condemn us because we're doing the best we can. Seventeen billion people in the world causes problems that the people in your time didn't even consider."

"We had such great plans. Such great dreams. Travel to the stars. Help the overcrowding by immigration to the stars."

"There are problems with spaceflight," said Munday. "There are no inhabitable planets in our solar system. Venus is too hot and Mars too cold. And the nearest star would take eighty thousand years to get to."

The elevator arrived and Kent entered. As the doors closed, he asked, "Why not send them into the past?"

"When? A thousand years ago. Ten thousand? A million? What about changes? One person making the wrong move, stepping on the wrong animal, bending the wrong plant, and everything comes apart."

They continued the argument all the way to the traveler's quarters and down the hall to their room. Kent walked to the window and looked out. The city seemed so peaceful, so clean, so perfect.

Munday put a hand on his shoulder, but he shook it off. He faced her and said, "I don't know you."

"You know me. I didn't make the rules of the society just as you didn't make the rules of your own. Your time wasn't all that great. Brushfire wars, chemical weapons, governmental corruption, and people dying of hunger and AIDS and a hundred other diseases."

Kent was going to respond and then didn't. He realized that she was right. They had traded some things to eliminate others. No one had looked hungry, but then he hadn't seen that much. No one looked sick, but he hadn't been to a hospital. Given their attitude, there probably weren't many hospitals. If your illness was fatal, it was nature's way.

"I don't want to talk about it anymore," said Kent.

"Why? You finally see the logic of it?"

Kent stared at her. "Logic? No, I see no logic. I understand how it might have come about, but I don't see it as logic. You have excuses now for not solving the problems. It's nature's way. Don't interfere because nature will take her course."

Munday shrugged. "It's the way things are."

Kent almost laughed at that. They were standing in a building that housed a device for time travel. Munday had already said she understood the concepts. A minor change had rippling, far-reaching effects in the future. They didn't make changes now. Jackson had been horrified at the concept of changing the past. But the solution was obvious. Make a minor change that would affect the future so that an undesirable element dropped out. The attitude of noninvolvement, for example. Maybe a little change in 1977 would mean that people suddenly helped their fellows as they had done through history.

Kent looked at her and said, "You know we're going to have to fix this Custer thing."

"Sure," she said, nodding.

"It might affect this time."

"That was the reason we returned to Gettysburg," said Munday. "To put history on the right path."

"Your Jackson seems reluctant to do that now."

"He was reluctant to make changes before we went back. Afraid that unseen events would ripple forward. We have some of that now."

"Still, we have to make sure that time follows the right path, if we know what that path is."

"Of course."

Kent moved to the bed and sat down. "We didn't start this time traveling for change, you know. Dr. Tucker's original idea was to view the past only, not interact with it. The first group to time travel was not scientists. They were corporate people who hadn't thought things through.

Didn't understand that time change could ripple through the centuries."

Munday moved so that she stood in front of him. She reached out and touched his hair, running her fingers through it. "I know that."

"Maybe if we put history back, it'll make things better here, in the future."

"Or make them worse. Change for the sake of change is not always the best. Too often people wanted progress because they were told progress is good. Sometimes progress isn't."

"I think the problem," said Kent, "is that we've always had such great hopes for the future. The problems are solved and everyone is happy. Now I find that we've traded one set of problems for another."

"Welcome to the real world," she said.

"Not real yet," said Kent. "We still have a job to do."

"If Jackson will let you," she said. "If Jackson will let you."

ELEVEN

Jackson wasn't happy with the people from the past. He had received a report from the guards that Maddie Munday and Andy Kent had gotten out of the building and had apparently been downtown. They apparently had done nothing other than walk around, although there was a story about someone trying to save a drowning boy. Some of the others had slipped away from the traveler's quarters, exploring the building, and Brown had tried to walk out the front door before being turned back. They certainly weren't as docile as the people from his time.

Now, he was sitting in his office, with the facts of the Custer battle on his computer screen again, but he wasn't seeing them. He was trying to figure out his next move. It was obvious to him that the people did not and would not fit in with their society. The way they obeyed his instructions proved that. Even Munday, who claimed to be a member of this time, was a renegade. But, more importantly, they had done something in 1863 to purposefully change time and it affected him now. The question was, would it make more trouble to fix it, or was it best to leave everything alone.

It was a dilemma that he didn't want to deal with. The decision should rest in the hands of someone paid to make such decisions. It should be left to a politician who had campaigned for office and decision-making status. It should not be left to someone running a relatively low-level government project.

And even though he knew that the travelers were waiting for him in the debriefing room, he sat there, staring at the computer screen, trying to decide how important the change introduced had been. He waited while someone else made the decision that he refused to make.

Reading the material on the screen and comparing it with the data he'd learned from the night before, the change had very little in the way of ripple effects. Custer died five years later, but it seemed that with his assassination, history slipped back to the right path. A minor aberration that no one was aware of except the travelers, and now a few people around him.

A small message appeared at the top of his computer screen. He touched a key, dumping the Custer material from the memory, and keyed in the electronic mail. The message came up, written across the screen rapidly.

"Decision for return and repair has been left in your hands. Advise of decision before it is implemented."

It was signed, "Latham Holt Winthop, Scientific Advisor, United American Republics."

Short and sweet and threw it right back into his lap. Exactly the situation he didn't want. Turning off the computer without making a printout of the message, he stood. He glanced at his desk, at the window and the greenbelt beyond it, and left the office, heading up to the debriefing room.

When he arrived, he saw that the travelers, dressed in the standard jumpsuits, were growing impatient. The remains of a breakfast were scattered on the table. Some kind of powdered eggs and reconstituted orange juice. There had been no coffee and no meat products.

Jackson sat down at the head of the table without a word. He saw that Sarah Hampton was sitting away from the group, watching them. They were all watching him.

"I think," said Jackson, "that the first order of business should be a complete report on your activities at the Battle of Gettysburg." He glanced over to Hampton and said, "Sarah, I think I'd like this recorded."

"Certainly."

Brown looked at Munday, waiting for her to start but when she said nothing, he spoke up. "We were dispatched from this time . . ."

"You mean this building here?" interrupted Jackson.

Brown turned to Munday for help. She said, "Yes and

no. There are minor changes here. Little things that aren't of much importance, but changes nonetheless. But we were dispatched from here."

"Yes," said Jackson slowly, as if digesting the information.

"But," said Munday, reading the situation and changing the direction of it, "the changes were necessary. History had taken a real strange turn because of meddling at Gettysburg."

"So you decided to meddle some more," said Jackson.

"We had to," said Munday. "It was a decision made by the Scientific Advisory Board."

"I didn't know that," said Brown.

"There are many things you don't know," said Jackson. "Now, what happened at Gettysburg?"

Brown began a detailed discussion of Gettysburg and how, according to the history he knew, the Union won. After they moved from 1836 Texas, into the future, they learned that Gettysburg had been radically altered. The future was a nightmare with Nazi Germany dominating the world. That was not meant to be, so they were sent to Gettysburg where an obvious change had been introduced. The job had been to ensure a Union victory.

He told it all, from the moment they arrived, until they left. He talked about the progress of the battle and the discovery of where the change had been introduced. In fact, they had learned the method of the change, and they eradicated it.

"Apparently our actions in 1863 caused a ripple change in 1876," finished Brown.

"Yes," said Jackson.

"Then you agree?"

He sat back, tented his fingers under his chin, and asked, "Why don't you brief me on the Little Bighorn? As you understand it."

Brown looked at the other members of his team. Most of them had a military background and were familiar with the more famous battles. Kent, Cunningham, and Andross were scientists sucked along on the first trip by accident, although both Kent and Cunningham had served in Vietnam. But, none of them, his people or the scientist, volunteered to speak.

"George Armstrong Custer and about three hundred men from the Seventh U.S. Cavalry were killed on June 25, 1876 when they attacked a numerically superior force of Dakota Indians made up of various tribes of the Sioux Nation, the Cheyenne, and the Arapahoe. Half the regiment, under the command of Major Marcus A. Reno, survived, holding a bluff for two days."

"How did it happen?" asked Jackson.

"If you mean, how did Custer and the five companies die, no one knows for sure. All the soldiers were killed and the Indians, when interviewed after the battle, told the soldiers what they thought they wanted to hear. The Indian survivors were afraid of retribution."

Now Kent interrupted. "This discussion is ridiculous. There is only one thing to do. We've got to go back and fix this because we created it."

"I don't know," said Jackson quietly, as if thinking about it. "As near as we can tell, this Custer episode is close to the natural time line. He took the place of Garfield on the ticket and was killed before he had a chance to do much. At that point, time rippled back to normal."

"Then you admit," said Kent, "that there is a normal, natural time line and we're not on it."

"That hasn't been demonstrated," said Jackson. "We have detected a few aberrations but nothing extraordinary. What we have here, in this time, is close to what we would have without your meddling." The message he'd received from the science advisor flashed in front of his eyes at that point. It was his decision to make, one way or the other.

Munday leaned forward, her hands on the table. "If we are aware of an aberration caused by our interference, I think we're obligated to repair the damage."

"Yes," agreed Jackson, taking a deep breath. "However, the question becomes whether the aberration is sufficiently annoying to warrant action by us. By trying to repair the damage, as you call it, we might make things worse. You've already admitted that this was caused by your attempts to repair a situation at Gettysburg."

"But we could make things better," said Kent. "We've moved closer to the original line."

"Well," said Jackson, "I think there comes a point where the benefits are far outweighed by the possible bad effects. We might have reached a point where it is better to leave well enough alone."

"No," said Brown. "We started this whole thing by accident at the Alamo. We didn't know what we were doing. We made some changes at Gettysburg that brought us closer to where we should be. I think a careful change, involving only a few people, might get us back on the right path."

"You do have a point," said Jackson. "And now that you understand how the smallest careless act in the past can affect the future, maybe you're right too. Maybe we should make a final effort to put history back the way we found it. Providing that you are extremely careful once you're into the alternate temporal environment."

Brown looked at his people again. "I'd want to take Thompson, Kent, and Baily. A minimum team."

"And Munday," said Jackson quickly.

"She's not one of my original team."

"No, but if you're going to travel on our equipment, and use our facilities, I want one of my people with you."

"You said that you didn't know her."

Jackson nodded slightly. "Obviously she's one of our travelers. Her equipment proves that and knowledge of the building proves that. Since you've worked with her, it seemed logical to assign her to you. To make sure that you do not violate your directives."

"I have no objections," said Munday.

"There you go," said Jackson.

"All right," said Brown. "We'll need costumes and weapons and some equipment. Maps of the area and an itinerary based on the current facts."

"Of course," said Jackson, "but you don't have to tell me my job. I know it."

Now Hampton spoke up. "We can have the briefing and field equipment ready in two hours. Another hour to study the maps and formulate a plan. Call it a four o'clock shoot."

"Wait a minute," said Brown. "One minute you're objecting to the idea and the next you're running at full bore."

Jackson smiled. "This isn't your typical bureaucracy. And I was confirming that you understood the ramifications of travel into the past and of changes made there. The decision about your trip has been made." He grinned slightly and didn't tell Brown that the decision hadn't been made until that moment. The choice had been left to him and he suddenly made it. The mission was a go.

"Then we need some time," said Brown.

"For what?"

Brown fell silent and could think of nothing. "I don't know," he said, shrugged. "Decompression. Getting used to the idea."

Jackson stood up. "I'll want to see you in my office to go over the maps and equipment lists, Brown. The rest of you can return to your quarters until summoned for the final briefings and the costume fittings later. Questions?"

"Why'd you change your mind so fast?" asked Kent.

"Didn't change my mind. I listened to all the facts and have decided that a mission to 1876 to correct an aberration, if handled carefully, is something that should be done. It's something that we can do without endangering the current time line."

"Then it's a definite go," said Munday.

Jackson stared at her and then nodded. "That's right. It's a go."

TWELVE

At the last minute, Jackson decided not to use his office. Instead, he took Brown and Hampton to a lower level conference room. It was furnished like the other but had a keyboard hooked into the mainframe and had a holotank for the display of the information. There was a window, but the blinds were drawn, shutting out the sun.

Jackson took the operator's chair, pulled the keyboard close, and typed in his command. The words were suspended in the air, floating over the holotank as if displayed on a giant screen. They flashed, vanished, and were replaced with a map of the whole Montana Territory, including the region of Montana where the battle would be fought.

With everything set up, Jackson stood and moved to the holotank. He pointed and said, "Custer and the Seventh left Fort Abraham Lincoln on May 17, 1876, moving to the west. Overall command of the column, which included more than just the Seventh, was given to General Alfred Terry. They reached the Yellowstone River, moved to the southwest where they met with Colonel John Gibbon. On board the sternwheel, *Far West*, they discussed the tactics of finding the Indians."

Brown was familiar with all that. It was the history as he remembered it. There was no reason to interrupt, so he sat back and listened as Jackson continued.

"At the end of the meeting, Custer's regiment was broken off from Terry's column and sent south to follow a trail that Reno had found two weeks earlier. Terry and Gibbon would circle around, coming in from the northwest and Crook was coming from the south. The Indians should have been blocked, no matter what direction they took."

"Yes, yes," snapped Brown, suddenly impatient. "Crook was attacked on June seventeenth, though no one on the *Far West* knew it. He had retreated south to lick his wounds."

"Then you know," said Jackson, "that everyone was supposed to meet on the Little Bighorn on June twenty-sixth."

"Yes. And that Custer force-marched south, driving his men so that the Seventh would gain all the glory."

Jackson nodded and moved to the keyboard. He typed for a moment and the map dissolved, disintegrating into flashing lights. Colored snow seemed to fall, and then began to solidify. The map now showed the whole of the Custer battlefield from the extreme eastern side near Ash Crek to the western end of the Indian village.

Again Jackson situated himself so that he could point down at the map. "About noon, the regiment reached this point. Custer was aware that Indian scouts knew of his movements. He was afraid that the Indians would escape. A group of thirty or forty Indians appeared suddenly, fired a few shots at the regiment, and then fled. Custer led the Seventh forward, chasing those men."

Brown realized immediately that this was the point where history diverged. It seemed that the Sioux were using the tactic that had worked so well ten years earlier when they had attacked, surrounded, and massacred Captain William J. Fetterman's small command in Wyoming.

"The chase lasted for more than two hours, the Indians never outdistancing the cavalrymen and the soldiers never quite able to close the gap. Custer let the column string out during the chase and finally halted it on the bluffs overlooking the Indian village."

Jackson moved around to the far end of the tank. He walked through the map, his shadow obliterating it until he was clear of it. Now he pointed and said, "Crazy Horse and the Indians poured from the village, firing rifles and using their bows. L Company, in the rear, took the brunt of the first attack and were almost wiped out. The survivors joined the rest of the regiment as they established a defensive position on the hilltop."

Now Brown held up a hand. "That's enough," he said.

"But I can detail the battle as it progressed, including Custer's attack into the Indian position about dusk."

"No need. I've seen enough. The problem here is that Custer never splits his regiment. He is forced to keep it together and it's the strength of the whole regiment, along with gaining the high ground, that allows him to survive."

Jackson looked surprised. "Then you already know what needs to be done?"

"Certainly. We have to ensure that Custer splits the regiment into three battalions. As long as he does that, he won't have the manpower to hold off the Sioux, especially if he's caught in the open."

Jackson rubbed his face. "How do you plan to get him to split the regiment?"

Now Brown stood and moved to the map. He pointed to Ash Creek and said, "This is the point the braves appear to taunt him. My people, with automatic weapons, ought to be able to turn the Indians. Without them coming at him, Custer will split his force as he's supposed to. Once we've got the Indians stopped, we can punch out."

"Okay, okay," said Jackson. He returned to his computer but typed nothing. "According to your version, no one with Custer survived to tell the tale."

Brown looked at the man. "That's correct. It's one of the things that has fascinated soldiers and scholars since the battle ended."

"Then," said Jackson, "if we return history to the proper time line, a lot of questions about the Custer battle will again be unanswered. Your soldiers and scholars will be trying to answer those questions."

"Which may be the reason that the fascination in the battle has endured for decades. People wonder how an officer can lead his men into a fight they have no prayer of winning. It may be the reason that we can sit here and discuss it intelligently. Everyone knows something about the battle."

"Granted, but we now have the opportunity to answer those questions. You and your people will be in a position to see what happens to Custer and all his men."

Brown laughed at the suggestion. "I've got one question for you. Just how do we see what happens to Custer and survive to report back here?"

Jackson was silent for a moment and then said, "That is a problem, isn't it?"

"Yeah," said Brown. "I would think so."

"Maybe we'll think of something."

"If you don't," said Brown quietly, "don't count on us getting the information for you."

Jackson sat quietly and then said, "I'll get back to you later."

"All right." Brown stood and left the conference room.

As soon as the door was closed, Hampton said, "If you send him back in time to make a change, you know what that means?"

Jackson turned, touched the keyboard, and cleared the memory. He then shut down the unit and rocked back in his chair. The chore finished, he said, "What does it mean?"

She laughed once. It was a short, snorting sound that was without humor. "We'll be affected by the change. Just as we were when they changed Gettysburg."

Jackson was quiet for a moment. Neither he nor Hampton knew about the change. As far as they knew, the world had always been the way it was now. They could remember nothing different, though Munday and the others told them that a major change had been introduced.

He understood her fear though. A change would be made and they wouldn't know. Their lives would be altered radically and there would be nothing they could do about it. Jackson felt his belly grow cold, an icy hand grabbing his stomach.

"We'll make a control shoot," he said suddenly.

"A what?"

"A control shoot. You and I into 1950 where we'll be protected from the change. Let it pass over us and then return here."

She nodded then. "I could live with that." She knew that hiding out in 1950 would protect them because changes did not affect the world until after time travel had been invented. It was one of those strange paradoxes. The people of 1950 knew one history and it remained the same no matter what happened in the past where the travelers played.

"We both could live with it," said Jackson. "Now, we've got a great deal of work to do before we push Brown and his people through. We'd better get to it."

"Certainly," she said. Her voice was stronger now that Jackson had decided there should be a control shoot.

THIRTEEN

With the briefing over, Brown walked back up to the traveler's quarters. Thompson was in the room watching a program on the holotank. There were half a dozen foot-high naked people running around on some kind of super game board. She glanced up at Brown and said, "It's a reverse striptease. The first one to put on all his clothes wins."

"Fine."

She saw that he was worried about something and turned off the program. She faced him and asked, "What's wrong?"

Brown sat down on the bed and stared at the floor. "There's something going on here that I don't understand. That Jackson fellow seems to be talking out of both sides of his mouth."

"Meaning?"

"That's just it. I don't know." He looked up at her. "One minute Jackson is talking about changing the past and affecting the future and the next he is planning for our return to the past."

"So?" said Thompson.

"I don't know but it seems if your overriding policy is to observe but not interfere, he should be denying us permission to go."

Thompson looked out the window, down on the city that seemed to be alive with people. At home, she could have stood in an office building and looked at the street and not seen many people outside in the middle of the day. The streets here were swarming with people. They didn't seem to have destinations. They were milling around, as if waiting for something to open, as if waiting for the lines to shrink rather than stand in them.

Finally she turned and said, "You remember the discussion we had at the Alamo so very long ago?"

"About the ethics of changing the past to fit your own personal needs? About the power available to those who controlled the time travel process?"

"Yes. Now maybe we're seeing the corrupting influence of it. Jackson has realized the power he has."

"But he has to be careful or he'll make a change that adversely affects him. He's not like Lewis who hadn't thought through the time travel possibilities. Jackson knows what can happen." He shook his head. "I don't think Jackson is grabbing at power though. He doesn't seem to be thinking in that direction."

Thompson said, "I'm sure that he's thought about it. He knows how to protect himself. And I wouldn't be surprised if he had made some computer projections in an attempt to learn what the ramifications of this minor alteration would be."

Brown rubbed a hand through his hair. "He can't have much data to work with. It'd have to be highly speculative."

"Certainly. But, if he can compare the histories of various time lines he would have some idea. We know that books written before time travel was invented show the history as it should have been brought forward and written. If he can pinpoint the change, then he'd be able to figure out how to stop it."

"We don't know that he is aware of all that," said Brown.

"The last time we were here, before we went to Gettysburg, Jackson was aware of all that. Since he still works with time travel, I would assume that he knows how to protect himself."

Brown felt his head begin to spin. It would be so simple to begin arguing in circles because time travel allowed that. Each argument turned in on itself so that logic became impossible to identify. One couldn't return to the past to kill his own grandfather because that would eliminate him from the time line, except that he would have to exist to return or his grandfather wouldn't be killed and he would exist to go do it.

Brown rubbed his temples and then said, "Computer projections might not tell the whole story. We had Dennison introducing wholesale changes. The computer model wouldn't be able to account for that."

Thompson shrugged. "Then the only solution is to keep a close eye on Jackson. See what his moves are, if you're that worried about him."

"I planned on that." He stood up and said, "We'd better collect the others and get down to costuming."

The five of them met near the elevator. As they entered, Brown slipped close to Munday and said, "I'd like to ask you a question."

"Go ahead."

"What do you know about Jackson?"

She looked up at the man and then closed her eyes. "You have to remember," she said, opening them again, "that the Jackson I knew was the one who sent us into the past to make the change. This man is the product of a different environment. He seems to be the same but he's different."

"That's a big help."

She shrugged. "What do you want me to say? The man I knew was raised in a world where war was a threat almost always. This is a more peaceful world. From the little I've seen, there haven't been that many societal changes, except there is no longer a Nazi threat."

The elevator stopped and the door opened. They stepped out and moved down the hallway. Outside the costuming room, they stopped. Brown hesitated and asked Munday, "Any reason we shouldn't do this?"

"Again, how should I know? It seems to be right and puts history back on course, but who's to say if it benefits the majority of the people."

Brown shrugged, still bothered by Jackson and still not

sure why. He opened the door and the five of them moved into the costuming room where a single woman, scissors in her hand, turned to face them.

"Welcome," she said.

FOURTEEN

The control room overlooking the shoot chamber was bright with light. Each of the technician's positions had been filled with Jackson himself sitting in the supervisor's chair. Hampton stood behind him, watching him as he worked. They were preparing the transfer, plugging in the coordinates, the time references, and the terrain data. That finished, Jackson got out of the chair.

"All right, Sarah, let's see what's going on now." He glanced at the window that overlooked the conference room. Brown and his people were in it already. They were dressed in the rough clothes of the period. Brown wore cavalry britches and a blue cotton shirt that looked almost like a uniform. The others, including the women, wore faded blue jeans and cotton shirts. All had hats, pistols, belts, and carbines.

Jackson studied them for a moment and then moved to the conference room. He sat down at the head of the table while Hampton stood off behind him, waiting. Jackson then nodded and said, "We're coming up on time. Let's get this taken care of."

Brown wiped at the sweat on his face. "Go ahead."

"Computer analysis of the situation suggests that the best time and place for you to appear is June twenty-second near the riverboat, *Far West*. There will be a conference held by the principals, meaning Custer, Gibbon, and Terry, to discuss the tactics and the strategies."

"We can't just blow in there," said Kent.

"No, of course not." Jackson picked up a bound computer printout that was lying on the table. "However, the Army will be searching for information about the enemy. If you, as civilians, suggest you know where the main Sioux

66

village is located, I believe Custer will want you with him."

"That gets us down to the Little Bighorn," said Brown, "but we're attached to Custer and unable to prevent the decoys from getting close to the main column."

Jackson nodded and held up a hand. "Then maybe two of you should appear at the *Far West* while the others stay hidden to operate as a separate unit."

"Three people to stop the decoys?" asked Baily.

"Look," snapped Jackson. "The important thing is to make sure that Custer divides his command. We wanted people with him as observers so that we could learn what happened during the battle."

"Now wait a minute," said Baily, his voice rising. "Everyone with Custer gets killed."

"If you'll wait just a moment," said Jackson, "we'll brief you on the entire situation." He turned to Hampton and pointed at the rear table.

As she lifted up a small, round, dull object, Jackson said, "We know that Custer and all who ride with him are going to die in the battle. This self-contained camera will float on the air currents for more than three hours. When Custer sends the final message to Benteen, this should be launched and used to track him through the battle. It'll photograph the scene on microfilm and it'll transmit video pictures to a receiver four or five miles away."

"Who will be carrying the receiver?" asked Brown.

"It can be secured in a saddlebag. It's small, almost invisible." Jackson pulled a saddlebag out of the equipment pile and showed them the receiver stuck into the bottom of it. He then took the device and showed them how to activate it. "Simple," he said, letting it float up, away from his hand.

Brown laughed. He gestured at his clothes and the modified weapons they carried. "Articles of the past so that we blend in. Now you're giving us a device that can't possibly be disguised."

"But who, in that period, would be able to tell anyone what it is. As long as it is recovered, there is no problem."

Brown took the map and looked at it. "I suppose that we

could accompany Custer as far as Medicine Tail Coulee. Then, we could slip away with the scouts and return to the others. Once there, and after we've received the pictures, we could initiate the retrieval and be out."

"The important thing," said Jackson, "is to get the decoys stopped so that history follows the right course. After that, you need to worry about getting the information."

Brown turned so that he was facing the others. He pushed the map toward them and then outlined his ideas on the subject. They'd want to stay in the background, and given their knowledge of the Indian locations, they could lead Custer to the points he wanted to be. They already knew exactly where the Indians were. They could talk about signs and trails and hunting parties, all of which could lead right to the Little Bighorn. Enough information so that Custer would want them around.

They looked at the plan. It was a simple one, but then there didn't have to be anything complicated about it. In and out and if they got into trouble, they could always flee to the future with no one being the wiser.

When Brown finished and his people were done asking their questions, Jackson asked, "Is everyone here ready?"

"Already?" asked Baily.

"Is there any reason to delay? You've been well fed, had a good night's sleep, and have been thoroughly briefed . . ."

"Briefed," said Baily. "We still need to be briefed."

"About what?" asked Jackson. "The map there shows you everything you need to know. Colonel Brown knows the history of the battle, and the task is a simple one that could be accomplished in an hour."

"Except we're going in three days early," said Brown. "Three days from the conference on the *Far West* to the battle."

"All right," said Jackson. "What more do you need to know?"

Brown shrugged and Baily shook his head. Finally he asked, "Won't Custer object to the women?"

"He took women along on his campaigns to cook and

clean for him. If they don't get in the way, there won't be a problem. If there is, leave them behind and we can retrieve them." Jackson laughed. "I know that you all have time traveled before, but you have to remember that a mistake made is not as permanent as it was once. Punch out and we can start again."

"Fine," said Brown. He looked into each of the faces around the table. "Anyone have anything to say?"

There weren't any responses. There really was nothing more to say. The plan was simple and had been laid out. They had been to costuming and gotten their clothes. Jackson had provided them with a nonfatal way of learning what happened to Custer after Martini left him with the message for Benteen. There wasn't anything else to discuss.

"If there isn't anything else," said Jackson. "Let's get going." He stood up and then waited. When the travelers were on their feet, Jackson glanced at Hampton. "Take them down to the shoot chamber and get them ready to punch out."

"Certainly." She waited as Jackson turned and headed into the main control room.

"You know," said Baily, "he could have wished us good luck before he left."

Hampton grinned and said, "He never does. Thinks it inspires bad luck. However, if it'll make you happy, I'll wish you good luck."

"Thank you, I think," said Baily.

They collected the gear that had been brought to the conference room, divided it up. There were weapons, modern weapons that had been modified to look like the standards of the time, canteens holding water, pocket watches, compasses, and ammunition. With it divided, they left the conference room and used a set of stairs to take them down a short flight so that they could enter the bowl-shaped shoot chamber. Hampton opened the hatch, spinning the wheel there.

Before they entered, Hampton looked at Munday. "Maddie? You got the retrieval bracelet?"

"Certainly."

"And you remember how to use it?"

"I managed to use it to get us back here, didn't I?"

"Yes, I suppose you did." Hampton stared at Munday and then said, "I know that I'm supposed to know you, but I really don't remember a thing about you. It's like you didn't exist until yesterday."

Munday laughed. "If this goes well, we can have this discussion again."

"I suppose so." She paled at the suggestion and turned her attention quickly to the whole group. "Anyway, good luck to you all."

Brown ducked and entered the shoot chamber. He stopped in the center of it and glanced up at the window. He lifted a hand to wave but no one there seemed interested in him, his people, or what they were doing. He dropped some of his equipment to the floor and turned to watch the others.

Hampton watched them all enter too, and then closed the door, spinning the wheel until the green light came on telling her that the door was secured. She waited and the light went to amber because they were beginning the sequence for the shoot. With that, she turned and rushed back up the stairs.

She entered the control room just as Jackson inserted his key into the lock switch, turning it one position. He looked at the technician on his left and nodded.

The man took a notebook from the rack and opened it to the first page that was protected by acetate. He used a felt-tip pen to mark off the steps and then said, "Main Temporal Sequence activated."

Jackson didn't respond. He turned a knob and flipped a series of switches near him. "Set one. Ready for level six."

"Power supply to full tap."

"Set to full tap," echoed Jackson.

"Coming up on power level and five minutes." The technician checked the dials to his right and said, "Initiate main sequence."

"Main sequence initiated. Cross over to level seven."

The technician flipped a switch and then watched as the technician to his right ran through a series of checks and then glanced at the warning lights using a thumb to flip switches. When he finished, he nodded.

"Cross over completed."

"Power levels at the ready."

Jackson twisted his key to the second position and said, "We're at level eight. Activate temporal lock."

"We're activated," said the technician staring at the LED in front of him.

"Check temporal chamber seal and sound the warning horn."

"Chamber sealed."

"I have a green board," said Jackson.

"Green board," said the first technician.

"Green board," said the second.

"Green boards all around. Prepare to launch." He turned the key to the last position and said, "Launch."

Behind the window was a golden flash and a bright light that seemed to solidify near the ceiling. It slowly descended and the people in the chamber were wrapped in the light. They sparkled for a moment and then vanished.

Jackson returned the key to the first position and pulled it free. He then glanced at the clock off to the right. "That's got it. Jerry, prepare for a second shoot to begin in thirty minutes."

"What the hell?" he asked.

"The control shoot."

He shook his head and said, "I don't know about a control shoot. Nobody anywhere said a damned thing about a control shoot."

"Of course not," said Jackson. "But it's authorized. You can call up to the advisory board, if that will satisfy you. You'll operate as supervisor as Sarah and I travel to 1950 Denver, Colorado." He wanted to say more but knew that if he kept talking, it would sound as if he were making it up as he was going along.

"What will you be doing in Denver?"

Jackson took a deep breath and exhaled slowly. "I'll, we'll be in the libraries and in the bookstores, surveying the literature of the time making sure that we haven't screwed up the whole time line."

"We've never done that before," said Jerry.

"Of course not, but this is a special case."

"Thirty minutes?" asked Jerry.

"Gives us enough time to get up to costuming for a change and then get down to the chamber. You can run up to the ready levels and then wait."

"Certainly," he said. "We have a chance for a cup of coffee?"

"A quick one," said Jackson. He stood up and looked at Hampton. "You ready?"

"I'm right behind you," she said.

FIFTEEN

As the hatch was closed, Brown turned and looked at the people with him. Munday sat down in the center of the floor near the pile of equipment, her forehead on her knees and her eyes closed. Before he could say a word, the golden glow of time travel exploded up near the top of the chamber and then slowly settled over them, obscuring the walls and the window of the control room.

Brown was aware of the trip starting. He was beginning to understand the sensations involved. A dizziness, as if he were on a roller coaster that was not moving but the horizon and ground around him was. He reached out as the walls shimmered and disappeared and the days took on the qualities of an erratic strobe.

All at once they stopped and the air around him heated rapidly. The sky was a bright blue, an intense color that almost hurt his eyes. Brown wasn't aware of the trip ending, but slowly realized that they were no longer moving. He took a deep breath and felt the heat that was broiling the Montana Territory. He wiped the beads of sweat from his face and then turned to the people with him.

"Everyone okay?"

There was silence and then Munday nodded. "I'm fine." She stood up and brushed at the dust on the seat of her pants.

Brown looked around. They were standing on a prairie covered with light scrub and green, ankle-high grass. There was a stand of cottonwood trees on the horizon. A bird windmilled overhead. Other than that single bird, the land seemed to be empty of animal life.

"Horses," said Baily. "We didn't think of horses."

Brown shrugged. "We popped into Gettysburg and

73

walked to our destination. We didn't need horses there."

"Because they put us down on the battlefield," responded Baily.

Munday unfolded the map she had brought. She glanced to the right and left and then to the front. She turned the map around and around. "This doesn't tell me a thing."

Brown took it and smiled. "There are landmarks all around if you understand them." He pointed to a stream and the steep bluffs on the other side of it. "See that. Now look at the map and you see a stream and you can see the way the elevation marks are stacked. That could be the bluff that we see there."

"Or it could be somewhere else," said Munday. "It's not very distinctive."

"So you look for other things. We can see a rise over there with a distinctive shape. That's right here. Then, we have a gentle slope that flattens out into a plateau. That puts us right here."

"Okay," said Munday.

"And, it means that we have to head in that direction, three, maybe four miles to find the Yellowstone River. An hour or two and no more."

Baily moved forward and then grinned. "Told you we hadn't thought this through. We should have brought some food."

"Except that in an hour we'll reach the Yellowstone that has all the fish we can eat, if we want. If we've got the date right, the Army will be there with everything we could ever need. It's not like there are no people around here."

"Then let's get going."

"Before we move," said Brown, "let's remember that there are Indians around here. No indications that any of them were this far north, but let's be careful."

"Shit," said Baily. "This is ridiculous."

"Take the point and keep your eyes open."

"Yes, sir," said Baily.

"Kent, bring up the rear."

"Of course."

Baily moved out, walking slowly at first, but then picking up the pace. He led them down into a wide, green valley, through a thin forest, and across a stream that was no more than a foot deep and fifty yards wide. They crossed it easily, then Baily turned, crouched, and drank. He splashed his face and then stood up.

"Additional water is supplied," said Brown.

"I still don't think we should have hit the field without the proper supplies," repeated Baily.

"Hey," said Thompson, "you don't pack a lunch to head downtown for shopping. Besides, you didn't open your mouth when you had the chance."

"Okay," said Baily. "Are we ready?"

"Go," said Brown.

They moved out of the forest then and up the gentle slope. It was hot, mid-morning, and the dust hung heavy in the air. A light breeze stirred it, creating dust devils, but it did nothing to break the heat. They reached the crest of the hill and halted again. Baily wiped away his sweat and then turned.

The rest of the people caught up with him and then sat down, except Brown who stood, turning slowly, searching for signs of the Army or the Indians. From the distance came a babble of voices. There was a cloud of dust.

"I think that the Army is over the next rise," said Brown. "Maybe two miles. Probably less."

"Then let's get going," said Kent.

"What's the hurry?" asked Munday.

Kent wiped his face and said, "I don't like feeling this exposed."

"Knowing full well," said Munday, "that the Indians are not close."

"Makes no difference."

"Andy is right," said Brown. "I'll feel better when we catch up with the Army. Give us some protection. We are exposed out here."

"Then let's go," said Munday.

Again Baily took the lead. They descended into the shallow valley, across the floor, and then up the hill. They reached the top and stopped. Spread out on the banks of the river below them, surrounding the riverboat moored there, was one of the largest Army camps that any of them

had seen. White shelter halves creating tents for the enlisted soldiers. To the right there was a huge herd of
horses, many of them brown, but dozens gray or black or
white.

"Jesus," said Baily. "Look at them all."

Brown took a deep breath and then said, "Told you we'd
be here in an hour or so."

"Now what?" asked Thompson.

"We go down and see how history is doing."

SIXTEEN

Jackson met Hampton outside the chamber where a green light burned. He looked at her costume, a dress from the early 1950s that had broad shoulders, a tight jacket cinched at the waist, and a long narrow skirt that reached nearly to her ankles. On her feet were black pumps with thin black straps.

His own clothing looked no less ridiculous. A double-breasted suit with wide shoulders, pants cut straight so that the legs looked like pillars, a wide hand-painted tie with a wood duck on it, black and white wingtip shoes, and a fedora that could be pulled down over his eyes, if he felt the need to hide his face.

"You look smashing," said Hampton, trying hard not to laugh at him.

Jackson wanted to repay the compliment, but she actually looked good in the clothes. He merely looked funny.

"We've about ten minutes."

"You get us any money?"

Jackson pulled a wallet out of the inside pocket of his jacket and waved it at her before flipping it open. "Two hundred dollars in the local currency. More than enough for three days in the field."

She took his hand, almost as if she were a teenager on a first date. "I'm ready."

Jackson pulled his hand free and opened the hatch. He let her climb in first. The narrow skirt made it awkward because the bottom of the hatch was two feet above the floor. She hiked the skirt up, over her knees, showing her thighs, and entered. Jackson followed her in and then looked up at the window of the control room. Jerry was there watching. Jackson pointed at him and then held a thumb up, telling Jerry that they were ready to go.

Hampton closed the hatch and then stepped to the center of the chamber. "I'd sit down," she said, "but I don't think I could ever get back up."

"I wouldn't look," said Jackson seriously.

"Really?"

"Of course not." He grinned then.

She shrugged and stood up straight, looking uncomfortable. Jackson slipped to the floor and crossed his legs Indian fashion. He watched the window, saw the heads of the technicians as they ran through the sequences. When the golden glow engulfed them, he stood up and took Hampton's hand.

"Where we scheduled to appear?"

"Little park close to the state capital, just off Broadway and looking down Colfax."

"Right out in public?"

"More or less," said Jackson. But then, before he could elaborate, they began to slip through time, the days rolling into the nights and everything beginning to flash like the flapping of a huge black wing.

They stopped suddenly and Jackson stumbled once before he caught his balance. He shook his head and then opened his eyes wide. Around him was the city of Denver, just as it should have been. Cars on the streets, roaring and honking. People, pedestrians, moving along the sidewalks. No one seemed to notice their sudden arrival, though they scared a flock of pigeons which flapped away.

Hampton lifted a hand to her forehead and seemed to sway. "You okay?" asked Jackson.

"It's the stop," she said. "I'm used to the acceleration, but the stop gets to me every time."

Jackson guided her to a bench and they sat down, facing a series of columns with only part of a wall. It looked like the ruins of a Greek temple, except it was in downtown Denver.

Trying to take her mind off the sudden motion sickness, he said, "Notice how the streets are angled. Comes from the beginnings of Denver when a rival city existed close to it. The town leaders didn't want it to look as if they were part of Denver so they laid out their streets at an angle. Down over there, hidden by the trees and a few buildings, is the Denver mint."

"Wonderful," she said.

He sat down beside her and said, "When you're feeling better, we'll go find a hotel and then a bookstore. Take a look at the modern history."

She had to smile. "You really going to do that?"

"Hey," said Jackson, "I have to make it look good. You might be able to see through my excuse because you helped plan this, but we have to return with the proper books. Besides, what else are you going to do?"

"We could go to the mountains and look down on the lights of the city."

"Why?"

"Because we're here and have the opportunity to do it. Because no one else from our time has the opportunity to do it and we shouldn't waste it. Because the mountains are there, open to the public."

Jackson looked at her and then shook his head. "We have to be careful, you know. We interact too much, too often, with too many people and we risk an accidental change in the future. It's the last thing we want to do."

"I know," she said. The color came back to her face. She was no longer pale. She seemed to be stronger. "Maybe we should get going."

"We have plenty of time," he said, not realizing how true the words were.

SEVENTEEN

Bob Cunningham sat in the dayroomlike area near the elevators and watched the holotank as he waited for something to happen. A light rain was streaking the windows that overlooked the city. Mary Jo Andross—a tall, skinny woman who had once worn her hair long, but who had chopped it short after her trips into the past—dropped onto the couch beside him and said, "We should be thinking about a way to get back to our own time."

Cunningham turned to look at her and then laughed. "You know, in all the confusion, I hadn't really thought about that. We get out of 1836 Texas and almost immediately we're in 1863 Pennsylvania. Now, part of the team is in 1876 and not one of us has thought to demand a trip back to our own time."

"They shouldn't object to that," said Andross, "because anything we do would be something we did."

Again Cunningham laughed. "A confusing statement, but one I understand. We couldn't adversely affect the future because it's our home time. That might be just the argument to use."

"What is?"

"Our mere separation from our own time could affect the time line . . ."

"But it hasn't so far," said Andross.

"Because we still have the capability of returning," he said. Suddenly he stood up and snapped his fingers. "That's right, as long as we can return, history won't change. We have to get back, plugged into our own time, close to the moment we left, or history is going to be affected."

Andross rocked back and looked up at him. "Then we have to go back."

"No way around it."

"But there are only a few of us here, now. Others were killed at the Alamo. There is no way they can return to their own time."

"Okay," said Cunningham slowly as he thought about that. "Okay. Let's look at this carefully. Could we remedy the situation? Possibly, but that seems unlikely. Could it mean that their disappearance from one point in the time line has no real effect on the whole? More likely."

"Meaning," said Andross, "that the selection process for the corporate employees, designed to select single, unattached people, inadvertently had a secondary benefit of taking only those people who wouldn't cause a ripple in the time line."

"That would be true for all of them, except, you, me, and Andy." He sat down and leaned back so that he was staring up at the ceiling. "Except Andy is now in 1876 trying to hook up with Custer's column."

"If he gets killed there, that could cause some problems."

"And Brown too," said Cunningham. "His selection wasn't quite the same as the others. His death could cause real trouble."

"He won't get killed." Andross smiled. "They all know what's going to happen. They can avoid it."

"So what are you going to do?" she asked.

"I think that we, you and I, should meet with the leaders here, the officials, and let them in on what we believe. Suggest that returning us to our own time is in their best interests."

"We should wait for Andy to return."

"Why?"

Andross shrugged. "I don't know. It just seems that it should be something we do together. We got into this mess together and maybe we should get out of it together."

"I don't think that's necessary. We can get the wheels in motion and when he gets back here, we'll be ready to punch out."

"If we remember what we've done," she said. "If his change doesn't mess up our minds."

"They only effect of that will be that we don't remember that for a brief time Custer was the winner at the Little Bighorn. We won't know why they returned to the past. But we'll certainly remember wanting to go home."

"All right then," said Andross. "That's what we should do. It beats sitting around up here, waiting for fate to take charge of us."

"Exactly my point," said Cunningham. He stood up. "Let's get at it."

EIGHTEEN

They stayed on the hilltop, looking down at the Army camp for a long time. The soldiers were milling around, as if resting after several days of hard marching. The flags and guidons flapped in the breeze and the horses were stirring, creating a cloud of dust that drifted to the east on the breeze. There were pickets out, but they didn't seem to be interested in what was happening around them. Several of them were dozing.

"Shouldn't we go on down?" asked Baily.

"Of course," said Brown, but still he hesitated. Like many soldiers, he had been fascinated by the Battle of the Little Bighorn and by Custer. He'd watched Errol Flynn make Custer look like the boy next door, good almost to a fault. He'd read of a Custer who was an egocentric maniac who never once thought of his men. He was a lucky man who had survived a number of blind charges only to have the very last fail him. Now Baily wanted to get him down the hill to meet the man in person.

"Well?" said Baily.

"Maybe some of us should stay here," ventured Brown.

"For what purpose?" asked Munday. "We're all going to be down there eventually."

"Just thinking out loud," said Brown.

"Let's go," said Baily.

"All right," agreed Brown. "But take it easy. Remember, these men are hunting Indians and might be a little trigger-happy."

Baily nodded and started down the hill slowly. He held his rifle cradled in his arms so that it was obvious that he had no hostile intent. The others spread out behind him so that they wouldn't all be caught in a cross fire should one break out.

Halfway down the hill, someone yelled, "Halt."

Baily stopped and turned toward the sound. "Where are you?" he called.

A soldier dressed in blue with corporal stripes, also blue, stepped out in the open. "Who are you?"

Baily glanced to the rear, at Brown, and he shrugged. There was no reason not to tell the soldier his real name. "Pete Baily. With information that Colonel Custer or one of the officers might find interesting."

"How do you know Custer is here?"

Baily realized that he had slipped there. There was no way he should have known. Then he shrugged and said, "I saw him earlier today." He turned and pointed back up the slope. "Saw him from up there."

"What's he look like?" said the man, thumbing back the hammer of his carbine. The barrel was still pointed, more or less, at the ground.

"Tall man, about six feet, a shade under. Short, light hair, blue eyes, and a ruddy face. Wearing buckskin britches and carrying a couple of pistols."

"Good enough," said the soldier. "Follow me." He turned and started toward the big Army camp.

Baily and the others followed along, staying ten or twelve yards behind, as if ready to run if something happened. They reached the first line of tents and were stopped again. This time a sergeant approached and they repeated the ritual.

Finally Baily lost his temper and shouted, "What do I look like. A Sioux?"

"What information do you have?" asked the sergeant, ignoring the question.

"We"—Baily turned and waved at the people with him— "found a large Indian trail leading toward the Little Bighorn."

"You come with me," said the sergeant. "The rest of you wait right here."

"Excuse me, Sergeant, but I discovered the trail," said Brown. "I examined it closely."

"Then you come instead. I only want one man. The rest can wait."

Brown moved forward and whispered to Baily. "Wait right here and keep the others corralled. Get some food since you seem concerned about that."

"Certainly."

Brown followed the sergeant through the camp until they came to the *Far West*. The conference having ended, the officers stood on the deck of the sternwheeler. It was smaller than he thought it would be, had three decks, the top one completely open. There were two smokestacks near the front and a pilothouse about a third of the way back with the name painted under the window where the pilot stood. It was drawn up close to the bank with several gangplanks, no more than two or three feet wide, leading up to it.

The officers, Terry, Gibbon, and Custer, stood on the ground, at the foot of one of the planks, talking. A small knot of officers and NCOs were close to them. They talked in low tones and then the group broke up, Custer turning to walk toward the cavalry camp.

"Colonel," said the sergeant approaching Custer, "this man claims to have intelligence on the Indians."

Custer stopped and Brown got his first good look at the man. Just as Baily said, he was a shade under six feet tall. His skin looked rough and ruddy. But it was his piercing blue eyes that drew attention. Brown had heard the term piercing before but had never known exactly what it had meant. Now he did. Custer's eyes seemed to bore through him.

"Come, man," said Custer. "What do you know?"

Brown wasn't intimidated by the man. But was surprised by his voice. It was higher than he would have thought and Custer stuttered slightly. Not much here now, where he was in complete command, but he'd heard it could become worse.

But then, Brown was talking to one of the mythical figures of the past. A second-rate general whose greatest battle had been a defeat where all the men with him died. A small battle when compared to some fought during the

Civil War. Yet there was something about the man. A magnetism about his person. He seemed slightly larger than life.

Brown pulled his eyes away from Custer's and said, "My people and I came across a huge trail a day or so ago. Hundreds, maybe thousands of Indian ponies all heading to the west."

"Indians don't have thousands of ponies. You exaggerate, man," said Custer.

"General," said Brown, "I don't exaggerate and I'll be more than happy to lead you to the trail. It was no more than a day old."

"How long ago did you find it?"

"Yesterday. We turned and came here immediately."

"On foot," said the sergeant.

Brown had to grin. Every time he thought that the rubes wouldn't understand him, someone proved he had powers of observation.

"We rode them into the ground," said Brown. "We were forced to leave them."

"You look clean," said Custer.

"Fell into a stream a mile or so from here. South of here. Cooled off and washed up."

"Hurrying to me, you stop to wash," said Custer.

Brown was about to respond and then remembered reading that Custer made a fetish of washing his hands. A hundred times a day. So Brown said, "Didn't take that long and I needed the drink."

Custer looked at the infantry sergeant. "You may return to your unit, Sergeant."

"Thank you, sir." He hurried off.

"Now," said Custer, "you come with me and take a look at my map. Show me this trail."

"Certainly, General. I have four people with me. For a horse apiece and some food, we'll ride with you. Show you where the Indians are hiding."

"I know where they are."

"Yes, sir."

"I turned down help from the Second Cavalry and four

Gatling guns. Why should I take you along?"

"Because the Second Cavalry and the Gatling guns don't know where the Sioux are. We do."

"Exactly?"

"Yes, sir. Exactly."

Custer stopped walking and asked, "How do you know?"

Brown shrugged and said, "We followed the trail and saw the camp. You would not believe me if I told how large it was. Seems that every Plains tribe is there. Sioux and Cheyenne and Arapahoe. Thousands of them. Maybe three thousand warriors."

"The Seventh can handle anything that the savages throw at us."

Brown wanted to tell him that it wouldn't handle them, but didn't say a word.

Custer moved into his camp and found a lieutenant. Brown didn't know who it was. History had not been kind to the lieutenants of Custer's regiment. Three of them would vanish in the fight. Jack Sturgis, whose father was the regiment's colonel, but who was assigned to duty in St. Louis, leaving Custer in tactical command, also disappeared, although bloody clothing belonging to him was later found.

Custer said, "I want you to take this man to find his companions and bring them here. Find them horses and see to it they are fed."

"Yes, sir."

They walked off as Custer had the bugler sound officer's call. Several of the officers, including Reno and Benteen, appeared then.

"Looks like you'll be moving out right away," said Brown.

"I'm afraid so," said the lieutenant. He was a pale man, looking as if he had bitten off more than he could chew. He was a frightened young man.

"What's your name?" asked Brown.

"Sturgis, sir."

"Well, Lieutenant Sturgis, you're about to ride out to

glory." Brown felt like a hypocrite saying it, but he couldn't tell the youngster, no more than twenty-two or twenty-three, that he was going to be killed in three days.

As they reached the others, Sturgis said, "Yes, sir, that's what I'm afraid of."

NINETEEN

Sturgis and Brown collected the others and moved over to where the Seventh Cavalry pack train was standing. Dozens of mules were loaded with the food, ammunition, and the supplies that the six hundred men of the regiment would need during the long campaign. Sturgis made sure that each of Brown's people had a horse and a cavalry saddle. If he suspected that two of the "men" were women, he didn't let on. Maybe he thought they were boys, or maybe he didn't care.

He led them back to the Seventh area where the men were mounting up, getting ready to move out. Custer was sitting astride his big sorrel, Vic. With him were the other leaders of the expedition, Gibbon and Terry. Sturgis led the new people closer, taking up a position in the rear while the Seventh passed in review.

As the last of the men rode by, Custer made ready to join them. Gibbon called out, "Now, don't be greedy, Custer, as there are Indians enough for all of us. Wait for us."

Custer moved off, waving, and called back, "I won't!" His stutter was more pronounced than it had been earlier.

As Custer charged after the front of the column, now stirring a cloud of dust, Sturgis yelled, "Come on. They'll leave us behind." He spurred his horse.

They caught Custer about thirty minutes later as the column climbed one hill and rode down into the valley. They followed the Rosebud, men dropping out frequently to water their horses. It wasn't a well-disciplined march at that point. There was an air of gaiety about it. The men were singing and joking and playing tricks on one another.

Custer seemed not to notice any of it. His eyes were on the horizon, as if he knew where the Indians were and could see them already. Custer turned in the saddle as they approached. He nodded in greeting and then said, "Scouts are out now, looking for the enemy."

Brown rode close and said, "We follow the Rosebud and then turn east and we'll find them."

"Good," snapped Custer. "We'll show them exactly what the Army can do. It won't be like Fetterman. This time we'll be victorious."

Brown shot a glance at the others around him, riding close. Behind them was the head of the column with their American flags and cavalry guidons. The regimental colors, the huge flag used during ceremonies, had been left at Fort Lincoln along with the band. Custer wanted to travel fast and he wanted to travel quiet.

"How far to that trail?" asked Custer.

"A ways, General."

"At camp tonight I want you to meet with the scouts and tell them what you know."

"Of course."

"Then tomorrow, you ride out with them. Take them to where the Indians can be found."

Brown nodded and thought quickly. According to everything he knew, the next day would be the twenty-third. Nothing would happen that day. They were still three days from the fight.

They traveled rapidly the rest of the day, making twelve miles before camping. Custer had told the men that he would select the site and he did, designating the company areas and placing the pickets himself.

Brown and his band stayed close together, away from the main body of the column, riding on the west side, outside the cloud of dust that was caused by the hooves of the horses and pack animals. The day was hot, the sun blistering.

When they stopped, Custer had a tent erected and then had his bugler sound officer's call. Brown looked toward the tent and said, "I think I'd better attend that. The rest of you wait here."

Munday looked at him and then said, "Be careful what

you say. Too much said and it could affect the future."

"All these men are going to be dead in three days," said Baily.

"No!" said Munday forcibly. "Only half the regiment will die at the Little Bighorn. You have to remember that. Reno and Benteen, two of the most senior officers, will survive, as will most of the commanders of the seven companies not with Custer." She turned and looked at Brown. "You have to be careful what you say in there."

"I understand that," said Brown. He nodded at them and then began the slow walk up the slight slope. He reached the tent, found a private standing guard.

"Officers only," said the private.

"I believe the General will want to hear what I have to say," said Brown.

Just then an officer peeked out and said, "The man is authorized to enter."

"Yes, sir."

Brown pushed the flap to the side and stepped into the tent. A large white thing with a makeshift table was in the center holding a map of the Montana Territory. Brown noticed that Custer was nervous, ill-at-ease. He paced in the confined space, the officers scrambling out of his way.

Two of them, captains, sat on the cot, watching. The others were crowded around the table. Benteen stood in the rear of the pack, as far from Custer as he could get. There was one scout, Lonesome Charley Reynolds.

"Now that we're all here," said Custer, "there are some things I want to say. No bugle calls except in an emergency. All orders will be cleared with me, personally. I will select the campsites and decide when we break camp."

He turned, walked to the rear, and then came back, leaning on the table. "I refused the offer of a battalion from the Second Cavalry. Our own regiment can handle everything the Sioux could throw at us. I want all the glory for the Seventh."

He waited, but no one said a word. "I refused the Gatling guns. They would slow us down. They're clumsy, top-heavy, and aren't that valuable in a cavalry charge. For defense, they make some sense. For us they would be useless."

He looked into the faces of each of his men. He stood up and said, "If we maintain our faith in the regiment, if we maintain our pride, then there is nothing we can't accomplish. We will be facing some of the finest light cavalry in the world, but they don't understand firepower or massing of troops."

Now he looked at Brown and said, "This man has told us there are two or three thousand warriors waiting for us up ahead. Official estimates suggest no more than fifteen hundred. It doesn't matter, our regiment, the Seventh, can deal with fifteen hundred or three thousand.

"Mister Brown," said Custer, "look at our map here and tell me right where we can find the enemy."

Brown moved forward and glanced at the map. It wasn't as accurate as the maps he had, but then, he needed to keep those hidden. The battlefield was already marked on them. Still, the names of the major rivers and streams were shown.

"There," he said, pointing to where the north fork and the south fork joined the Little Bighorn. "Right there."

"Reynolds?"

The man shrugged. He had one arm in a sling from an infected thumb. He was a man of medium height with blue-gray eyes and stood erect. He had the air of the aristocracy, but seemed to be shy.

"Could be. Indications are they were heading in that direction."

Custer turned then to the rest of his officers. "Have you understood my instructions?"

They nodded and murmured.

"Then you are all dismissed. Mister Brown, I want you and Charley to remain behind."

When the others had filed out, Custer sat down on the cot and looked up. "You are a mystery, Mister Brown. An educated man who understands the Indians well enough to predict where we can find them."

"Yes, General."

"I want Charley to ask you a few questions, if you don't mind."

"Go ahead."

Reynolds looked at Brown and held out two arrows. "Which is Sioux and which is Cheyenne?"

Brown looked at them, saw the blue paint on one and pointed at it. "Cheyenne."

"How do you know?"

"Cheyenne always paint their arrows blue, or carve wavy lines on them to represent water."

"What color do the Sioux paint their lances?"

"Sioux don't carry lances."

"Tell me about this country."

Brown looked down at Custer who was watching him intently, his blue eyes seeming to shine. Brown turned his attention back to Reynolds.

"To the southwest, over the Bighorn Mountains is a place of hot water that smells of rotten eggs. Streams of water erupt into the sky." He stopped talking, trying to remember other things about the country that he could describe. He could tell of Devil's Tower, almost due south of them, but couldn't call it that. He couldn't tell them of Cody, Wyoming, at the entrance to Yellowstone National Park because those things didn't exist.

"The Bozeman Trail is south of here, moving to the north and the west through northern Wyoming Territory. You've the Powder River there. Off to the east are the Black Hills."

Reynolds held up his hand and nodded. "Man seems to know what he's talking about. I've been to Yellowstone and seen the hot springs. Every one of the things he says is true. I've seen it too."

"Mister Brown," said Custer, sitting forward and grasping the edge of his cot. "What's your game?"

"I'm afraid that I don't understand."

"Just what are you doing here?"

"Oh." Brown looked at the map and then said, "Sioux attacked my camp and killed a number of my men. Fell on us without a warning and murdered my fellows. I want to get even."

"I don't buy that," said Custer. "You look to be too smart for revenge."

"While the Sioux are loose, looting and killing, no one is safe."

"That is too true." Custer stood up. "Thank you, Mister Brown. I will consult with you later. Please stay close to the camp."

"Yes, General," said Brown. He left the tent, knowing that Custer was suspicious of him. There was nothing he could do about that. As long as Custer listened at the crucial minute and as long as they could prevent the decoys from trying to draw him into the trap, everything would be fine. They could stop the charge from being made and history would revert to the path it was meant to follow.

He found the others and said, "We're in for now. Custer is going to let us ride along."

"That isn't exactly good news," said Kent.

"No, but that's the way it is. Now, let's just be careful for the next forty-eight hours and we'll be out of here."

TWENTY

Jackson and Hampton walked up Colfax Avenue and found a small hotel that rented rooms by the week. The important thing was that they had a small kitchenette where they could cook their meals. Jackson had insisted on that because it meant they could eat in the room, away from the restaurants where they would have to interact with the locals. The less of the people they saw, the less the chance they could inadvertently change time.

They had gone up to the room quietly, aware of the clerk watching them. They'd brought no luggage with them, Jackson telling the clerk that it was in a locker at the bus station. The man had nodded, but hadn't believed him.

Up in the room, Hampton had dropped onto the bed and kicked off her shoes. She hiked her skirt up so that she could reach her feet and massage them. She wasn't used to wearing high heels and the shoes weren't the most comfortable made.

Jackson had walked around, appalled at the primitive conditions. The rug on the floor was dusty. The bed looked to have been well used and sagged in the center. The refrigerator was a white box that looked like someone had attached a tub to the top. There was a giant radio and when Jackson turned it on, it took thirty seconds to warm up.

He crouched in front of it and spun the dial, listening to the whooping and the static of the thing. He heard tinny voices that rattled at the speakers. He found some music, the big band sound of swing.

"How long do we stay?" asked Hampton.

"Three days at the least," said Jackson, standing. He turned and watched as she massaged her feet. "Three days here and then retrieval. That way Brown and his people will have made their change and we'll be safe."

"And until then we hide up here."

Jackson sat down in the chair. It was well stuffed, but was stiff. There were fabric-covered arms that were frayed. He leaned over and looked up, inside the lamp shade of the floor lamp, and turned on the light. The gray from the daylight was beginning to fade.

"The very least we can do," said Jackson, "is observe the local people for the research section. Buy some newspapers and nonfiction books. Maybe a few magazines that have lots of pictures. Other than that, yes, we should hide out up here."

Hampton laid back and laced her hands under her head. She stared up at the ceiling. "So what are we going to do for three days?"

Jackson knew what she was hinting at, but decided to make it hard on her. "I would think we could review the material we find, making sure that it is important to take it back." He closed his eyes as if thinking. "Wish they had video tape in this era. We could buy some of those."

"Great," she said.

Jackson laughed then. "It's only for three days. You can do three days standing on your head. Even if we were out in the woods, three days is nothing."

She sat up and tugged at the hem of her skirt, jerking it down, over her knees. "Three days," she repeated.

"Right now," said Jackson, "I think we'd better get us some food and find a couple of newspapers. Tomorrow, we can search for a bookstore or two and then make a few purchases."

"Fine," she said.

Jackson stood up and moved to the door. "You coming?"

She found her shoes and put them on. She stood up, swaying slightly, showing that she wasn't used to the balancing act that high heels required.

"Ready," she said.

They walked down the dimly lighted hallway, her heels tapping on the hardwood of the floor. They reached the elevator and waited for it. As the door opened, the man seated by the controls warned, "Step down, please."

"Lobby," said Jackson.

They descended in silence and when they stopped, the man opened the door and said, "Step up, please."

They left the hotel and moved out onto the street. With the sun gone, it was chilly. A cold breeze whipped by them, pushing along the dead leaves that had been ripped off the trees. Hampton slipped closer to Jackson.

"We should have brought coats."

"Can't we buy something?" asked Hampton.

"Sure."

They walked along Colfax, watching the traffic swirl around them. A horn blared once. Tires squealed, but there was no crash. No sound of smashing glass or twisting of metal.

They kept walking, ducked into a store to warm up and then out again. They found a small grocery and bought enough food for the night. Soups and bread and jelly. Although meat was considered a luxury in the future, they were revolted by the meat counter. It reeked of copper. There was liver and brains and kidney available. Neither of them wanted to eat the internal organs of animals.

Jackson paid for it and headed toward the door. Hampton bought a newspaper. "Back to the room now?" she asked.

"For tonight," said Jackson.

They left the store. Now it was dark, except for the pools of light created by the street lamps. It chased some of the gloom, but not all of it. Hampton moved to the very edge of the sidewalk so that she was close to the street. The shadows scared her.

Jackson laughed at her. "Nothing's going to happen here, in the middle of the city."

They walked in silence, and then a shadow moved. Hampton stopped and looked, gasping. A man—wearing a dark overcoat, the collar turned up, and a hat, the brim pulled down—stepped out in front of them. He took his hand out of his pocket, showing them his gun.

"You stop right there," said the man.

"Okay," said Jackson.

"I want your money, your rings, and your watches."

"Please," said Hampton.

"Just give me your money and your jewelry and no one will get hurt."

Jackson dropped the bag and said, "We'd better do as he says."

"Now you're thinking."

TWENTY-ONE

The day dawned hot. Custer was up with the sun, quietly ordering the men to break camp. They had a long way to go before they would find the enemy. There was just enough time for some hardtack and coffee boiled over a small fire.

Within minutes, they had broken camp, packed everything, saddled the horses, and were ready. Custer, along with the scouts, was at the head of the column. Brown and his people were again off to one side.

Custer gave the command and the scouts broke toward the front, rushing forward, the hooves of their horses stirring up a cloud of dust. The air was filled with it and the smell of wild plum, roses, and crabapple.

Moments later, the whole column began to snake forward. One minute they were all sitting quietly, the horses nervous, and the next they were on the move, the air filled with the quiet noise of creaking leather, horses, and a rattling of equipment. Custer had demanded they move in silence, and yet nearly seven hundred men, along with their horses and supply train, could not.

The direction of march was south, on the western bank of the Rosebud. Compared to the day before, the first few minutes was a leisurely walk to give the scouts a chance to get ahead of them, the flankers a chance to get into position on either side of the column, and to let the rear guard drop off.

Brown found the whole process fascinating. He'd seen enough movies, watched enough military operations, and read enough manuals to understand what was happening, but everything seemed to show the column already in motion. The front company moving at a steady pace while the rear was either at a standstill or galloping to catch up.

And they weren't quiet. The men were calling to one another, whistling, and, periodically, there was a bugle call, Custer's orders against it forgotten. But Brown knew, as anyone who had been involved in a large unit movement, there was no way to keep six hundred men quiet. They made noise. The horses made noise. The equipment made noise.

Not to mention the cloud of alkaline dust stirred by the horses. Even walking along, the horses' hooves kicked up clouds of it. The rear of the column, with its sudden dashes to catch up, stirred even more dust so that it looked as if a part of the prairie had caught fire.

At midmorning one of the scouts returned and Custer halted the regiment. Brown and his people slipped closer to Custer as the scout talked about a small trail that had led to the remains of countless wickiups and lodge circles.

"Big village. Sioux. Grass all around gone. Ponies."

"Did you find the line of march?" asked Custer.

The scout pointed toward the west. "That way. Bighorn Mountains."

Custer glanced at Brown and raised his voice slightly. "Your information seems to be good. So far."

Again they started, now angling to the southwest, to where the scouts had found the village. As they approached the village remains, Bloody Knife, one of Custer's scouts, rode out to meet them. He pointed out a rock carving near the encampment.

It showed two bulls, one smaller than the other. The larger bull seemed to have been shot while the smaller had been pierced by a lance.

Bloody Knife told Custer, "It say, 'Do not follow the Dakotas into the Bighorn country for they will turn and destroy you.'"

Custer stared at the rocks for a while, one hand stroking his chin. Finally he lifted a hand, took off his hat, and wiped the sweat from his face. "I am not frightened by the bravado of savages."

Again they pressed on, now the pace picked up. Custer knew the Indians were near. Signs of them were everywhere. There were the remains of the village. The signs of a giant pony herd that ate the grass from the hillsides like a plague of locusts. They had found a fresh scalp. It had been mounted on a stick, almost as if intended as another warning.

Farther up the Rosebud there were even more signs. The Crow scouts, including Bloody Knife, found more discarded trophies. A dozen scalps and the beards of white men.

But most important was the trail. More than a mile wide, it looked as if the earth had been plowed. Each of the scouts stopped, climbed from his horse, and studied the ground. Each of them knew that it meant a huge party of Indians, thousands of them, had passed by.

They returned to the main column and told Custer what they had found. They had thought he would realize what it meant, but he didn't. Instead he saw that much more glory. A chance to break the back of all the Plains Indians at once.

Custer still pushed on, suddenly afraid that the Indians would escape him. He stayed at the head of the column, dashing off toward the horizon and then returning rapidly, at a gallop. He seemed full of energy while the rest of his men seemed to be dragging. They slumped in the saddles and prayed for a chance to rest, but Custer just urged them on, talking of a great victory and great glory.

Finally, having passed more abandoned campsites, now where the pony droppings were fresh, Custer knew they were close. At dusk, they halted again. The men spreading out, dropping to the ground exhausted. Custer had ordered no fires and no noise, afraid that the Sioux would be warned of their approach. The soldiers were too tired to care.

They rested fitfully, each man knowing what was about to happen. Brown and his people picked a camp near the tent used by Custer. They sat together and talked quietly. Brown was trying to figure out a strategy that would keep them all out of harm's way as they tried to keep Custer from leading the whole regiment against the Indians.

Brown sat on the ground, leaning forward. His body

ached from a day in the saddle and from the tension of knowing that the Seventh was riding to its doom. One word spoken to the right man at the right time would prevent the massacre, but that wasn't the reason he was there. He had to ensure that the Seventh rode into a battle, hopelessly outnumbered.

"It doesn't get easier," said Thompson, her voice hushed. "We keep ending up at these sort of times."

"Two days more," said Kent, picking up on her mood.

"Okay," said Brown. "I think we'd better think things through. Be sure that we understand what needs to be done and how to do it."

"What's to know?" said Baily.

"We need to separate ourselves from the column before noon on the twenty-fifth, stop the decoys, and then rejoin with Benteen."

Thompson shook her head. "I don't want a part of this. I really don't."

"There's nothing we can do about it now," said Munday. "Besides, it was you, or rather your people, who brought up the changes in history."

"Which doesn't mean we have to associate with men who are about to die," said Thompson.

"I don't want to hear any more talk like that," said Brown.

Thompson looked at him and said, "Why not? Half the men here believe they are going to die. One of the scouts was giving away his belongings, figuring he wasn't going to need them anymore."

Baily picked it up then. "And what about Custer himself? His little talk last night scared half the men who heard it. They don't understand his attitude. Some of them think that Custer believes he is going to die."

Brown was going to warn them again, but Sturgis arrived suddenly, interrupting them. He stood just outside their circle, as if waiting to be invited to join them.

"Sit down, Lieutenant."

"No, I don't have the time."

"Then what can we do for you?"

"I thought I'd better warn you that the general is going to want to leave here soon. Knows the hostiles are close and doesn't want them to get away."

"I don't think he's got to worry about that," said Baily.

"Meaning?" asked Sturgis.

Brown broke in. "There are signs that there are thousands of Sioux and Cheyenne around."

"The general has said the Seventh can handle them."

Brown shook his head. "It's good to have confidence in your troops, but not to the point of foolishness. Three thousand Sioux and Cheyenne are a formidable force."

Sturgis stared at Brown, their eyes locked. Finally he looked away and stood. "We can handle them."

"I'm sure you can," said Brown hastily. "The Seventh is the finest regiment in the cavalry."

"That's true," agreed Sturgis. "Just don't let the general hear you suggest that the Sioux can beat us under any circumstances."

"I know better than that."

Sturgis stood for a moment, looking down at them. He glanced at Thompson and Munday and then back at Brown. "Before we move out, I'll come back. The general has assigned me to you."

"That's fine," said Brown.

As Sturgis walked away, Thompson whispered, "What happens to him?"

"He dies with Custer and his five companies. He's the youngest of the officers and owes his appointment here to his father, the commander of the regiment."

"Wait a minute," said Baily. "I thought Custer was the commander."

Brown took a deep breath. "It's a strange situation. The commander is a colonel named Sturgis but he's assigned to recruiting duty in St. Louis. Custer has field command by virtue of being the senior officer with them."

"Sturgis must be thrilled with the arrangement," said Baily.

"Nothing he can do about it." Brown laughed. "It's a funny situation. Everyone thinks Custer was a general who commanded the Seventh. Instead he was a lieutenant colonel with only the tactical command."

There was a faint bugle call. Brown turned and looked back at the black mass of the Seventh Cavalry. "Guess it's time to move out again."

TWENTY-TWO

Jackson stood dumbfounded, staring down at the barrel of the gun held by the man. It was pointed directly at his stomach and didn't waver. The man wasn't a scared kid trying out armed robbery for the first time. He was a cool professional who had the situation in hand.

"I want your money and your jewelry," he said.

Hampton glanced at Jackson as if he had some idea about the situation. She stood rooted to the ground, her posture suddenly rigid, as if her body had turned to stone.

Time seemed to slow to a standstill. Jackson was aware of everything around him. The cold wind blowing down the street, the sound of the cars as they sped by, the noise from the city. A light flashed as a car turned, illuminating the man's face momentarily. As it vanished, he waved the gun.

"Now!"

There was nothing Jackson could do. Without looking at Hampton he peeled off his watch and handed it to the bandit. Knowing that he was giving up all the money they had in that time, he handed over his wallet. There wasn't much of substance in it because they hadn't seen a need to create an entire identity. It was just a place to carry the money.

"You, too, sister," said the crook.

Hampton handed over her watch, a ring, and a five-dollar bill. As the man grabbed it, he noticed the bracelet that she'd failed to remove.

"Come on, sister. All the jewelry."

"You have everything," she said.

"The trinket on your wrist."

"Oh, no," she said. "That's no jewelry..."

"I don't care what it is. I want it." To underscore his

105

point, he thumbed back the hammer of his weapon. "Now."

"Do it," said Jackson.

"But . . ."

"Do it. It's better than dying here and now. Give it to him." Jackson's eyes were focused on the robber. He was unaware of what they were discussing.

"But . . ."

"Lady," said the man, reaching out to grab at her.

She recoiled and then pushed up her sleeve, opening the retrieval bracelet. She slipped it off her wrist and handed it to the man.

With that the gunman whirled and sprinted down the alley. Jackson moved to follow him, entering it but then stopping suddenly. There was no light. A dark mass off to one side that smelled, even in the cold air, of rotting garbage. Someone or something kicked a tin can that clattered for a moment and then stopped.

Jackson stood there, in the entrance for a moment, trying to see something behind the darkness. Suddenly he was cold, the sweat of fear first bathing him and then drying in the breeze. He shivered and turned to face Hampton who came up behind him.

"Now what do we do?"

Jackson shrugged. "The room is paid for. We check out early, we'll have a little money."

"Not much," said Hampton.

Jackson turned and moved back to the street where the sack of groceries he'd dropped lay. He stooped down and began putting the items back in the bag.

"I don't see the money as that big a problem," he said calmly.

"Jesus," she snapped. "Screw the money. He took the retrieval bracelet. We've no way to get home."

Jackson felt his stomach grow icy. He looked up at her, into her face, now partially lit by the streetlight near them. He wanted to scream at her. He wanted to cry. His head whirled and he felt suddenly short of breath. The importance of the theft had just sunk in. He fell back, landing on his butt, unable to speak for a moment.

"We've got to find that man," said Jackson suddenly, turning to look into the alley again.

"How?"

"I don't know," snapped Jackson. "But we have to."

TWENTY-THREE

For the first few days they had been in the future, they had been guarded on the traveler's floor. No one had been allowed off except to attend the debriefings and the interviews, but then the guards began to get sloppy. Those who lived in the future no longer saw those who had come from the past as a threat to their way of life.

The guard who'd sat in the dayroom just off the elevator disappeared, and no one monitored the comings and goings of the travelers. Cunningham and Andross left the quarters and walked to the elevator. They took it downstairs, stopped on the main floor and walked to the front of the building.

Outside, they could see an expanse of lawn, the edges of it lined with palm trees and flowering bushes. There was a sidewalk that led to a gate where one man stood guard. He didn't seem to be concerned with the people who milled around on the sidewalk beyond him.

They watched that for a few minutes, not understanding it. So many people outside with nothing to do but walk around in the sunlight. No one was moving fast either. No one seemed to have a destination.

They left that and walked back to the elevators, passing the color photographs of history being made. A few of the pictures were next to copies of famous paintings that recorded the event before there were cameras and time travel. Now they could see how stylized the individual artists were and they could see how the painters had interpreted the scene. Rarely did the photograph look like the painting.

Downstairs, they walked along the hallway until they came to the conference room just outside the retrieval pit.

They opened the door, surprised that it wasn't locked, and entered. Through the glass at the far end, they could see the technicians working, see the big board that held a map of southern Montana in the region of the Rosebud and the Little Bighorn, and see the window that looked down on the shoot chamber.

Cunningham walked across the carpet, pulled out a chair, and dropped into it, studying the scene in front of him. As he watched, the map on the board changed, showing the downtown area of Denver. One of the technicians stood up, moved out of sight, and returned carrying a computer printout.

"What're they doing?" asked Andross.

"Hell, Mary Jo, how the hell should I know?" asked Cunningham. "Looks like they have more than one team out. Our people at the Little Bighorn and somebody in Denver."

"Doing what?"

"Studying the past," said Cunningham, shrugging. "What else would they be doing?"

Andross slid a chair around so that she could watch and sat down. As she did, one of the technicians looked out, into the conference room, and then turned away before Andross could wave at him.

There was a hurried conference and the man in the supervisor's chair turned, looked at them, and then stood up. He moved to the door, opened it, and said, "You people can't stay in here."

"Why not?" asked Cunningham.

"Because we're involved with some important work and we can't have interruptions."

"We weren't interrupting," said Andross. "We were sitting here watching."

The man shrugged and lifted his hands palms up, as if checking for rain. "Whatever. The point is, you can't remain in here."

Cunningham took a deep breath. Behind the man, he saw the board return to the view of Montana. One of the technicians used a keyboard and several points of light, grouped close together, appeared near the western bank of the Rosebud, but no longer very far from the Little Bighorn. The team was moving close to it. The battle was only a few hours in their future.

The supervisor said, "You're going to have to leave here now."

"Why?" asked Andross.

"Listen, if you're not involved in the shoot, then you're going to be a distraction."

"Hell," said Cunningham, "if it's that big a deal, we'll split. But first, we wanted to ask you about returning us to our own time."

"Can't do it," said the man automatically.

"Why?" asked Andross, beginning to sound like a broken record.

The man wiped a hand across his forehead, almost as if he was sweating, and then rubbed it on the front of his lab coat. "You can't return because you've already seen the future."

"So what?" said Cunningham.

"So a return to your own time, with the knowledge of what you've seen here, could adversely affect the course of history from that point."

"Possibly," said Andross. "But you're forgetting that our removal from our own time could also adversely affect the future from that point."

"Except that it hasn't," said the man.

"Because there is the possibility that we can return. You arbitrarily take that away and you may be altering the past in a harmful manner."

The man looked back into the control room, saw the board, and looked at the flashing lights on it. He then stuck his hands in the side pockets of his lab coat and said, "It's not my decision to make. Dr. Jackson will have to decide."

"Fine," said Cunningham. "He's a reasonable man and I'm sure that he'll understand the benefits of returning us to our own time. Where is he?"

Again the man looked at the big board. He pulled out a chair and sat down. "He's not available at the moment."

"That's no problem," said Andross. "We'll just wait until he is."

Again the man wiped his forehead, but now he was beginning to sweat. He glanced at the clock and then at the two time travelers.

"The truth is, Dr. Jackson has returned to 1950 for research. Retrieval for him isn't until tomorrow. There's really no reason for you to wait here."

Cunningham saw the reaction and asked, "There something that you're not telling us?"

"No, not at all. Listen, I've really got to get back to work. Please check in with us in the morning. Dr. Jackson will have to make the decision."

"Fine," said Cunningham. "Mind if we sit here quietly and watch?"

"You want to go home, you'd better not see anything more. Too much knowledge might have an adverse effect."

"All right," said Cunningham, standing. "I wouldn't want to jeopardize our chances of returning home by seeing anything more."

Andross joined him as he moved to the door. "Please tell Dr. Jackson we want to see him as soon as he returns."

"Certainly." The man moved toward the door.

Cunningham waited for Andross and then both of them left the conference room. As they reached the hall, Cunningham said, "There's something wrong in there."

"How do you know?"

"Didn't you see the way he began to sweat toward the end. Something big has happened and he's working overtime to keep it bottled up."

"But it's nothing that affects us," said Andross.

Cunningham stopped walking and looked back at the closed door and thought about the map of Montana. "Unless someone has already been killed."

"I don't know that much about the Custer massacre, but I don't think they get into it until the twenty-fifth of June."

"Which could be now," said Cunningham. Then he remembered that the marks on the map were still north and west of the battlefield. They hadn't reached it yet.

The man returned to the control room and slipped into his chair. He glanced over his shoulder to make sure that neither Cunningham nor Andross had returned. Satisfied that they were on their way back to the traveler's quarters, he ordered, "Switch back to 1950."

The map of Montana faded and the one of Denver came up again. He watched as the single blip moved along the streets of Denver, away from Colfax, moving toward the south.

"Bring up the aberration again."

There was a shifting as the map progressed backward. When it reached the point he wanted, he said, "Freeze. Now slowly, forward again."

They watched as the signal faded completely and then came back again. As it did, it began moving rapidly. "Comments," said the supervisor.

"Hampton took off the recall bracelet for some reason."

"I don't like it," said the man. "Why would she do that?"

"We could initiate a recall and ask her."

The supervisor turned to his computer screen and touched the keyboard. He shook his head once and said, "We can't initiate the recall now. Without a signal from their end, we don't know what might happen."

"We'd better do something," said one of the technicians.

"No, not until we get a recall signal."

"They might be in trouble."

"No," said the supervisor again. "If they need help, they'll give us a signal." He sat back and looked up at the map. As he did, the light there faded and the signal disappeared.

"Oh, shit," said one of the technicians. "That's not supposed to happen."

"Maybe they turned it off."

"Why?"

The man shrugged, still staring at the screen where the signal had been. "There is no reason to do that. Ever." But the signal was gone and that was the only thing he could think of. At least he hoped that it was what had happened.

TWENTY-FOUR

They were moving early on the twenty-fourth, Custer ordering the men to their saddles about four in the morning. He rode out, in front of the column, and then came back as the last of the men had broken camp. With the sun climbing high, the dry air filled with dust, the men were miserable. The horses were dragging, worn out from the forced march of the day before and unable to get sufficient rest. The sky was filled with insects that tortured the men and the horses. The march turned into a nightmare as the dust swirled around them, choking them and covering them all with a fine gray film.

Brown, along with his people, managed to stay off to the side where there was little dust. They only had to fight the heat and the insects and the long hours in the saddle. Sturgis rode out once to talk to them and then later Benteen left his company and rode over. He fell in with them, riding along in silence for a moment.

He was a man of average height and looked nothing like a warrior. He seemed almost too slight to be a soldier, with a look of gentleness about him. That was in stark contrast to his wild hair and fiery eyes. He looked almost like the stylized pictures of John Brown circulated prior to the Civil War. Brown knew he was a man of consuming passion who hated Custer for his desertion of Joel Elliott and the twenty men with him at the Battle of the Washita eight years earlier. It was hard to believe the man now riding near them was a professional killer and a professional soldier.

But then Brown looked into his eyes and saw something there that he had seen in the eyes of young men fresh from combat in Vietnam. They were old eyes that seemed to be

113

bottomless and maybe dead. Eyes that had seen too much too soon.

Finally Benteen looked over at them and said, "I'm afraid that I don't understand your role here. I don't understand why you're here."

Brown nodded and took off his hat. He wiped the sweat and dust from his face and said, "I'm afraid that we don't either. We had planned to give our information to the Army and let it go at that. Gain revenge without having to ride back into the heart of Indian country."

"But Custer fooled you."

"I don't know, Captain," said Brown. "I didn't expect to ride along, but then, I can't think of a safer place to be, surrounded by the Seventh Cavalry."

"But you talk about three thousand Indians out here in the biggest village ever."

Brown turned his full attention on Benteen. "There something on your mind, Captain?"

Benteen took a deep breath and then exhaled slowly, noisily. "We are pushing forward, with all possible haste, and I'm afraid that we're going to find the Indians. More than we think." He waved a hand at the horizon. "The signs are getting bigger and more frequent. We've passed a dozen campsites, each one larger than the last as the Indians join one another. There are hills where there is no grass."

"Captain," said Brown, "exactly what are you trying to tell me?"

"You look like a bright man. I shouldn't have to lay it all out for you, but here it is. You and your people should turn around and ride north. Find the Yellowstone River again and get out. Get to the riverboat and ride it to safety. This regiment is doomed."

"You surprise me, Captain."

Benteen shook his head. "You and your people have no reason to ride with us. It's not the grand crusade that Custer would lead you to believe. I don't know what he's trying to prove. Maybe he wants to show the world that he's the same George Custer who led all those cavalry charges in the war. Maybe he wants a great victory to regain his glory from ten years ago. I don't pretend to understand it but I know he's about to sacrifice this regiment to do it."

"Why do you stay?" asked Brown. "Knowing what you claim to know."

"Because there is no choice. I'm a soldier assigned to the Seventh and I will not desert it. My job is right here, along with the other soldiers."

"Well," said Brown, "we're going to ride along with you for a while longer."

"That's your choice, but don't say you weren't warned in advance." He turned his horse then and rode back toward his company.

Brown watched him go and then turned back to the people with him. He found it interesting that Benteen knew what was going to happen. During his years in the military, he'd seen the same thing and heard dozens of stories about men who knew their time was up. Some of them survived and laughed about it, others didn't. Now he was riding with a regiment that seemed to sense something dramatic was about to happen. The whole regiment, from the officers right down to the newest of the recruits, sensed that this expedition into the Montana Territory was not going to end in the same successful fashion as their other forays against the Indians.

Maybe it was the signs all around them. It was obvious to everyone that there were thousands of Indians nearby. The abandoned camps, the travois trails that had churned the earth, cutting it to a powder six inches deep and making it look like a recently plowed field. The hillsides were stripped of vegetation as the Indian ponies ate everything they could find.

And then Brown realized that they weren't passing a series of large camps, but a single camp that was so gigantic that it had stretched for miles. Every soldier of the Seventh had seen that, and everything else. Each of them had to know what it meant, and yet they kept riding forward, maybe because there was nothing else for them to do. Maybe because each of them believed his personal destiny was wrapped up in the guidons of the Seventh.

• • •

At dusk, they halted. The column was stretched out over several miles now. Those in the front nearly fell exhausted to the ground, forgetting about their horses, eating, or military discipline. Those in the rear still had a couple of hours of hard riding to reach the camp.

As he had done the night before, Custer called the officers together. As they approached, a sudden gust of wind caught the general's guidon and knocked it down. A lieutenant picked it up and jammed it back into the soft earth, but the wind knocked it down again. The lieutenant stood there, looking at the fallen guidon, as if it were something horrible, a sight that no human should have to see.

As Brown approached he heard one of the officers say, "Just one more bad sign. I don't like any of this."

When the officers, along with the scouts and Brown, had assembled, Custer moved to the table where he had spread his maps.

"Tomorrow," he said without preamble, "we should make contact with the hostiles."

He looked from face to face as if seeking approval from each of them, and then continued. "From this point, we will have to move faster if we're to prevent the savages from escaping. By attacking them from the east, we can drive them to the north into Terry or to the south into Crook if they flee."

"And if they stand and fight," asked one of the officers quietly.

Custer grinned. "Then we'll crush them under our feet and the Seventh will have the glory. The Seventh will have it all and not have to share it."

Benteen stood at the back of the group, as if he were afraid of getting too close to Custer. "What about our orders from General Terry?"

"Our orders," said Custer, "are to find and destroy the enemy. That is what we are going to do."

Custer then moved to the map and began to go over his plan. Until he got closer, he wouldn't know exactly what he wanted to do. They'd all have to remain flexible, ready to respond to the changing situation. He took out his watch and checked the time. To the assembled officers, he said,

"I want to be moving again inside of two hours."

"We'll be in violation of our orders," Benteen reminded him again.

Custer whirled to face the officer, his eyes flaring with anger. Then he smiled and said, "Great victories erase mediocre orders. No one will remember what our orders were in two days time." He fixed his gaze on Benteen. The captain stared back, watching until Custer was forced to look away. "Anything else?" he demanded.

No one had a word to say.

"Then we move out in two hours. You're all dismissed now."

Slowly the men filed out of the tent. Brown looked at the cavalry guidon again. He knew what its falling over meant. Custer was about to fall. And it seemed that the other men, those without knowledge of the future, were bothered by the omen. They all knew that it couldn't be good.

TWENTY-FIVE

They rode through the night. Custer had ordered the sabers boxed and left behind, afraid that the rattling of them would alert the hostiles. But as the dog-tired regiment rode from the Rosebud toward the Little Bighorn, they were making noise. Coffee cups rattling against fry pans. The creaking of leather of saddles and holsters. Metal rifle barrels against the leather of the saddle or metal of canteens. Not the quiet, nearly silent regiment slipping across the prairie to surprise and destroy the Indians but a noisy, tired regiment where every man except one prayed they wouldn't find the Indians.

Brown and his group had watched as the regiment mounted. When they finished, riding off toward the next horizon, he called his people together and looked into the tired, dirty faces of each of them.

"Fifteen, sixteen hours, and it all will be over. Now we've got to be very careful," Brown warned them.

Thompson slipped closer and asked, "How are we going to handle this?"

"We'll stay close to the head of the column and watch for the decoy. If it materializes, we'll destroy it. If not, we let Custer divide the regiment and then try to stick with Benteen. Once the regiment separates, we'll drop off, launch the little flying spy, and then head for the bluff where Reno will defend himself for two days."

"Can't we just leave the equipment on automatic and retrieve it in a couple of days?" asked Kent.

"The remote won't be able to follow the action," said Munday. "We can set it to record all in a specific location, but with the battle spread over more than four miles or so, there has to be some external control."

The first of the companies had mounted and was beginning to move off. Brown glanced at them and then said, "We have to stay alert and close together. If things go bad, we can always punch out."

Baily stood near his horse, the reins in his fist. He rubbed a hand over his face. "Maybe the thing to do is just get out once we know that Custer divides the regiment. There are some things that shouldn't be known. Mysteries add some spice to life."

"Always the romantic," said Thompson.

"No, not that. I just don't think that we need to risk our lives so that some academician sitting in an air-conditioned room can know exactly how the battle progressed."

"I'll have to agree with you, Pete," said Brown, "but now that we're here, we might as well see this thing all the way through."

"But we'll be careful," said Kent.

"Always," said Brown.

He swung up into the saddle and looked back at the small group of people. He'd started with more than thirty, arriving at the Alamo with them all. A few had been killed there and the rest had scattered through 1836 America. Then they had been recalled, some of them going to Gettysburg. Now, there were four of them about to ride into the valley of death that was known as the Little Bighorn.

Brown had a chill on his spine. The falling cavalry guidon suddenly scared him. He knew what it really meant, but wished he hadn't seen it happen. It was almost as if seeing it fall meant he would be there to see Custer and the regiment fall, and if that happened, he would be in great danger too.

He shook it off, forcing the thought from his mind. He looked at Thompson, and again felt the cold breath of death on the back of his neck.

"You ready," he asked her, not because he needed to know, but because the conversation would require him to concentrate on something else.

"All set." She climbed into the saddle to wait.

When everyone was mounted, Brown said, "We need to stay close to the front of the column from this moment on."

"Of course," said Baily.

They rode forward hurriedly, hearing the noise of a company in front of them. The night was dark, with a scattering of stars overhead, hard to see through the dust kicked up by the horses. There was no moon. There was no breeze. Just the rattling of the equipment and the swirling dust.

Brown slowed them and they fell in behind the lead unit. Custer was in front of them and the scouts were out, searching for a trail that would lead them to the Indian camp.

After three hours, Custer and the head of the column rode into a deep, wooded ravine. Custer slipped from the saddle and stood near an alkaline stream watching as the horses tried to drink. Some of the troopers removed the saddles and rubbed the backs of the animals with dried grass. Others sat down, wrapped the reins around their arms, and then stretched out to fall asleep.

Brown and his people stopped short of the ravine and looked back to where the rest of the column was lost in the darkness and the floating gray cloud of dust. It would be hours before they all reached the ravine.

"Now what?" asked Baily quietly.

"We'll rest for a while, moving out before eight in the morning. Custer will have reports from the scouts about the size of the Indian village."

A shape loomed out of the dark then. Sturgis, leading his horse, moved closer. "The general suggested that I remain close to you for the next couple of days."

"You're welcome to join us, Lieutenant," said Brown. He nodded at Thompson. "Maybe we should brew some coffee."

"The general has ordered us not to make fires tonight. We're too close to the enemy."

"Well, hell," said Baily, sitting down. "Then I'll drink a little of this water and go to sleep."

"Probably the thing for us all to do," said Sturgis. "Tomorrow is going to be busy."

"Then the general has learned that the Sioux are close?"

"Hell," said Sturgis, "the scouts have been telling us

that for two days. Mitch Bouyer said that there were more Indians than he'd ever seen in one place." Sturgis yawned, putting a hand up to cover his mouth. "Damn, I'm tired."

"It's been a long march," said Brown.

"You don't know the half of it. We've been on the move for six, seven weeks." He stopped talking and looked around as if afraid that the other officers might hear him. "These last few days have been even worse. The general seems determined to find the hostiles and eliminate them by himself."

There were things that Brown wanted to say then, but didn't. Knowing the fate of the man who sat in front of him, he couldn't talk about telling the grandchildren about the march. He couldn't say that in a few hours it would all be over, nor could he mention that the backbone of the Indian strength would be broken, even though Custer would lose the fight.

Instead, he said, "I'm getting pretty tired."

Sturgis took the hint. He stood up and said, "I'll check on you in the morning."

"Thank you, Lieutenant."

As Sturgis walked away, Tom Custer strolled over. He was made almost in the image of his brother. A stocky man with dark hair, but smaller than his brother. Brown was interested in meeting Tom because he was one of the few men to have won two Medals of Honor.

Custer crouched near him and stared up at him. "Got a question for you."

"Go ahead."

"Just what in the hell are you doing here? Once you gave us your intelligence, you could have ridden away."

Brown shook his head. "We had no horses. Besides, your brother wanted us to show him where we found the Indian trail."

"Nope," said Custer. "I don't buy that. You could have showed us, though we certainly don't need the help. There're signs all over the country and Varnum and his scouts claim we're getting close."

"What's your point?"

"I don't trust you."

"Well, hell, Captain, I don't like you either but that doesn't mean we plan to lead the Seventh into some kind of a trap set by the Sioux and the Cheyenne. Just what do you think we're going to do?"

"That I don't know. I just wanted you to know that I was going to keep an eye on you."

"Well, thank you, Captain. I appreciate it."

Tom Custer stood and then said, "I don't think you'll appreciate it for long." With that, he hurried away, disappearing into the gloom of the woods, heading toward his brother's tent.

"What was that all about?" asked Thompson.

"I don't know. But everyone is getting jumpy. They all feel it. Everyone knows something big is about to happen to them. Hell, they can see it. Signs are everywhere and more than one of them think the Indians are going to swarm all over them."

"Then why do they stay?"

"Where would they go?"

"Back along the line of march. They've seen that country. They could desert and no one would be the wiser."

Brown sat quietly for a moment and remembered the attitude of the soldiers he'd known. They complained about the way things were being run, complained about their orders, and complained about the hardships. But few of them ran in the face of danger. Not because they didn't want to run, but because they wouldn't leave their friends. Maybe it was an esprit de corps that kept them together, or maybe just a loyalty to a friend, but they didn't run. Especially when danger was facing them.

After the danger had passed, and while they were drinking toasts to their comrades who had died, each said the same thing. He was glad to have gone through it. Given a choice before, he would have opted out, but then, when it was over, he was glad to have done it.

That explained why these men, having come this far, and feeling that things were not going well for them, stayed with the regiment. There were stragglers, and there would be men who would slip away from Custer's five companies before the fight, but the vast majority of the men would ride into the valley with Custer and would die with him. As would two brothers, brother-in-law and his nephew.

"I guess I don't have a good answer for that," said Brown. "They stay because it's the only thing they can do."

"And we stay?"

"Because it's the only thing we can do."

"I hope it's not the last thing we do," she said quietly.

TWENTY-SIX

David Jackson sat in his hotel room and looked out on the darkened streets of 1950 Denver. A few cars were moving, their headlights bobbing along, flaring and then fading. There were people out walking, moving slowly, as if they had no real destination in the cold of the night. The stores were dark, but the bars were bright.

Hampton sat on the bed, staring at her feet. The groceries sat on the table where Jackson had set them after they returned to the room. Neither had been hungry. Both realized the problem they now faced. There was no way for them to return to the future because there was no way to initiate the recall. The crook had stolen their means of returning.

"What are we going to do?" she asked again. Her voice was low, tired, discouraged.

Jackson whirled and snapped, "You don't need to keep asking me that."

"You should have thought of this before. We should have thought of it. What happens to the traveler if he or she loses the recall bracelet?"

"It never came up. Everyone knows the importance of keeping the bracelet close. No one ever lost one before."

"Someone should have thought of it."

"Then why didn't you?" asked Jackson. He felt the anger spread through him like a white-hot fire. He wanted to leap the three feet that separated them and hit her. Slap her face and knock some sense into her. Or out of her. But then, controlling himself, he turned, looking out the window, and forced himself to relax.

"Okay," he said quietly, "we're doing ourselves no good

by snapping at each other. We've got to put our heads together and work out a plan."

"I don't want to be stuck in 1950," she said. "I don't know a thing about it. It's strange. Alien. And money. We don't have any money."

"Stop it," said Jackson forcibly. "You're worrying about trivia."

"Being stranded in this time frame is not trivia. Having no money and no prospect for earning any isn't trivia. We have no friends and there is nowhere we can go for help."

"Panic won't help either," said Jackson. He turned again and walked to the chair, sitting down. Hampton started to speak, but he waved at her, telling her to shut up for a moment. "Let me think."

"Go right ahead," she said sarcastically. She slipped to the rear so that she could rest her back against the headboard of the bed. She stared at the toes of her shoes with an intensity that suggested the answer to their problem was somehow written there, on them.

Jackson was quiet for several minutes and then said, "I read a story when I was a kid. A time traveler got trapped in the past and used the local media to help with his rescue. Put an ad in a magazine that only someone in the future would recognize. It was his call for help."

"What magazine?" asked Hampton.

"That's the problem. In the story there was only one magazine that could be used. We've thousands. Someone would have to know where to look to find it and they'd have to know we were in trouble to look. It's a great solution that doesn't apply for us."

Hampton sat up then, that story triggering a memory. "Hey, we could use the system that those others, Kent and Cunningham, used. Entrust a letter to a lawyer to be delivered in the far future. Address it to Davies or one of the others and tell them where we are."

"Okay," said Jackson. "That would work." He fell back in his chair. "But it's a long-term proposition that doesn't solve the immediate problem for us. We still have to live out our lives here."

"What?" said Hampton. She shook herself and added, "No we don't. All we have to do is tell them to pop in here and rescue us. In fact, we could tell them to rescue us in the next ten minutes, giving them this location." She sat back as if to wait for the rescue party.

"Only one problem with that," said Jackson. "We haven't written or sent the letter yet. We still have to do that. Then we have to wait for it to travel into the future in normal time. In other words, we live a full life here, in Denver. The rescue takes the form of a time change."

"No!" she said, nearly screaming. She doubled her fists and pounded on the bed. "No."

"Think about it," said Jackson calmly. "Right now we have no way to short-circuit time. We have to wait for the letter to get there. Then they change the past by meeting us at the designated time and place."

"Why don't we just build our own recall bracelet?" she asked suddenly.

Jackson rubbed a hand over his face. "Because some of the items used in it won't be invented for more than fifty years. There is no way to produce a powerpack without access to a radioactive isotope that won't be discovered for seventy years and we can't hurry the process because we'd have to alter the current state of physics and that would introduce changes that could affect the future."

"Oh hell," she said. "I should've let the robber shoot me when he had the chance."

"It's not nearly as bad as you believe," said Jackson.

"How can you say that? You've doomed me to a life in a primitive culture where everyone believes that the destiny of a woman is to get married and have babies. A woman who wants a career is an aberration in this time and she has to fight through a hundred roadblocks."

"In ten years it will be the 1960s and women will be allowed more freedom. Jobs will open up."

"And by 2000, women will be accepted into almost every career field, though the draft will still register only young men and the pay for women will only be ninety percent of that given to men."

"With your advanced knowledge of science, both physical and social, you should be able to create a few learned papers to work your way into academia," suggested Jackson.

"And tell them what? Explain particle beam physics to them? Tell them about the latest in laser surgery? Anything I do is going to change the future."

"Okay," said Jackson, realizing that she was going to object to everything he said. She wanted to complain and that was what she was going to do. Not make the best of a bad situation, but attempt to make it worse.

Jackson closed his eyes and steepled his fingers just under his chin. "There is one other thing that we might try. It's a long shot, but could get us out of here in three or four days, if it works."

She sat up then, excited. "What?"

"If the man who stole the retrieval bracelet accidentally activates the retrieval signal, they'll know that something has happened. If they send out a search party, they'd naturally start at our touchdown point. We'll need to go back to the park and wait to see if anyone arrives to pick us up."

"And if he decides the bracelet is worthless and throws it away?"

"Then there'll be no retrieval signal at all. After our itinerary expires, someone might send a search party to see what happened to us. Again, the logical place to start would be the park. We go back there."

Hampton sat up and swung her feet to the floor. She stood, smoothed down her skirt, and said, "Then let's go."

"Not now," said Jackson. "It's dark and it's cold."

"But we might miss them."

"No," said Jackson. "They'll try to set down at the same time of day as we did. Daylight hours. They'll be as logical about this as we are. We won't miss them."

Hampton sat there quietly and shook her head. Finally she said, "I can't believe that we didn't work all this out beforehand."

"It never came up," said Jackson. "But when we get back, a procedure will be written."

"So all we can do now is sit here and do nothing."

"Tonight, yes. Tomorrow, we head to the park, but we also write the letter."

"Fine," said Hampton, though it didn't look as if she was thrilled with the idea.

TWENTY-SEVEN

Just after dawn, Custer met with Varnum and the scouts while the rest of the regiment prepared to move out. Suddenly he changed his mind and allowed them cooking fires for brewing coffee and boiling the hardtack. It was as if the Sioux would no longer be able to see the smoke if the soldiers cooked their breakfast.

Brown tagged along as Custer followed Varnum to a spot west of the Little Bighorn. They climbed up a bluff to a point that stuck out, known as the Crow's Nest. As they approached the top, they got down and crawled forward on their bellies, trying to keep from silhouetting themselves against the brightening skyline. There were two or three of the other scouts there and Varnum held a hurried conversation with them.

Varnum pointed to the east where there was a brown hill. "There," said Varnum, whispering.

"What?" snapped Custer. "I don't see anything."

"There," said Varnum again. "That brown hill. Do you see it?"

"I see the hill, yes."

"And the strange brown color?" asked Varnum.

"What's so strange about the color?"

Varnum looked at Custer and then over at the scouts. "Spring grasses would be green. Hills should be green. Won't burn brown until late July and then it'll be a lighter brown. A dusty color."

"What in the hell are you talking about?" snapped Custer angrily.

"That's the pony herd."

"What?"

"That brown mass is the Indian pony herd. Largest I've

ever seen. Must be twenty, thirty thousand of them on that hillside. Gives you a feel for how large the village must be."

Custer stared, a hand shading his eyes, and then said, "I don't see anything."

Brown slipped forward and stared into the distance. There was a light haze that had filtered down the long valley looking almost like a light wood smoke from a thousand campfires. He glanced to the south, where the village should have been erected, but the lay of the land was in the way. No sign of the Sioux, Cheyenne, and Arapahoe, except for the pony herd massed on the side of the hill ten, twelve miles distant.

Bouyer crawled up to join them, first staring off into the distance and then back to Custer. Lowering his voice, he said, "Biggest damn village I ever saw."

"Where?" asked Custer.

"South of the Little Bighorn. So big I couldn't see the far end of it."

Custer, using binoculars borrowed from one of his officers, turned to search the ground in the south. Still he could see nothing of the Indians. He turned to look to the west at the brown hill and shook his head.

"I still don't see the ponies."

"They're there, General," said Brown. A hundred years after the battle, historians wouldn't be able to understand Custer's sudden inability to see the horses. Brown thought that he understood it. If the pony herd was as large as everyone said it was, there was going to be many more Indians than Custer wanted to meet.

Custer finally pulled his eyes from the binoculars and slipped to the rear so that the Crow's Nest was between them and the suspected Indian village in the valley below. He sat there for a moment, his elbows on his knees and the binoculars held in his left hand.

"I want the scouts to stay here and watch. Any change, I want to know about it immediately." He looked at Varnum. "You understand?"

"Yes, General."

"Mister Brown, I want you to stick close to me this morning."

"Certainly."

He slipped a little farther down the hill and then stood up, brushing at the rear of his buckskin pants with a hand. "Let's get back to the regiment and get them on the march. We've got ground to cover."

They hurried to the horses and Custer swung up into the saddle. He sat there for a moment and then said, "Gentlemen, we're going to make history today."

Brown pulled himself up into his horse and then glanced at the east. It was about four or five o'clock in the morning. There were less than twelve hours. Six or seven until the decoys would ride out to draw Custer into the ambush. If history continued to follow the wrong path.

They headed back to the regiment at a gallop. As they approached, one of the officers rode out and joined them. Custer didn't slack his pace, but called to the officer. "Let's get the regiment ready to move."

"Yes, sir."

Brown broke away then, riding toward where Thompson, Baily, Kent, and Munday waited for him. He saw them, first sitting around a small fire with Sturgis and then they stood up, turning to face him.

"Biggest damned pony herd on the face of the continent," said Brown as he swung down, out of the saddle, gasping for breath.

"Signs been there," said Sturgis. "What'd the general say about it?"

Brown looked straight at the young officer and shook his head. "Claimed he couldn't see them, but he has to realize what we're going up against. This is no Washita with the Cheyenne sleeping."

Suddenly the air was split with the sound of Boots and Saddles. Soldiers who had been drinking coffee or making breakfast dumped the coffee onto their fires and kicked at the embers. They broke camp quickly, assembling in company order. There were more commands, some of them shouted. The noise from the regiment grew and it was as if the orders for silence had suddenly been rescinded. No one cared if the Indians heard them. Maybe they all hoped the Indians would be alerted and would flee before they could get there.

Within minutes, they were ready to move. Brown, with his tiny band, moved forward, toward the headquarters unit. Custer sat there, waiting. Behind him were the six hundred men of the Seventh Cavalry, about to ride into history. Brown wished that he could record the event, photograph it, but couldn't. A camera used now would cause questions to be asked. Questions by men who would survive the fight to talk to the five civilian scouts that joined them at the Yellowstone. He didn't want to do anything else to complicate the future.

Custer stood up in the stirrups, turned to face the regiment, and put one hand back, on the rump of his horse. Satisfied that the men were ready, he waved a hand forward and then dropped back, into the saddle.

They started forward, and then stopped. To the right was a small cloud of rising dust and Custer was about to dispatch a patrol when two men came over the hill at a full gallop, riding straight for him.

Custer sat quietly, waiting as the two men, scouts who had been left behind with Varnum, rode up. They slid to a halt and one of them said, "We saw a group of Sioux moving downstream rapidly."

"They see you?" asked Custer.

"We don't think so, but they seem to be in a hurry. The lieutenant thinks they're going to warn the village. He thinks they spotted signs that we are close."

"Damn!" said Custer. "I was afraid of that." He looked to the rear, at the regiment and then back at the scouts. "How many?"

"Small party. No more'n fifteen."

"We're going to have to hurry or the hostiles will certainly escape."

"General," said Brown. "If they haven't detected the regiment by now, I doubt they will. You don't have to worry about the Indians escaping."

"What does that mean, sir?" demanded Custer.

"That it is impossible to move six hundred men as

quickly as we've moved without leaving considerable signs. The dust cloud we raise has to be visible for miles. They have to know that we're closing on them."

"All the more reason to hurry," said Custer.

"If they haven't run by now, they aren't going to," said Brown. "They'll be waiting." As he said it, he could have bitten his tongue. His job was to make sure that Custer rushed into the attack and suddenly he was advising caution.

"If they wait, they make our task easier," said Custer.

The lead scout pointed back, in the direction of the Crow's Nest. "We return."

"Go," said Custer. He then looked at Mitch Bouyer. "I think we've caught them."

"General, I think that if we pursue the hostiles, we won't survive until nightfall."

Custer laughed and asked, "Why do you say that?"

"The Crow have sung their death songs. They have given away their possessions. Hell, General, you've seen the signs yourself. We're chasing ten thousand hostiles."

"The Crow are old women, afraid of their shadows, afraid of each other, and afraid of the Sioux. The Crow have always been afraid of the Sioux."

Bouyer looked to the rear, at the column that was the Seventh Cavalry. "You've got a fine bunch of boys here, General, but I don't think it'll be enough."

"The largest Indian camp on the North American continent is ahead and I am going to attack it."

"Then many good men will not live to see the sun set tonight."

Custer turned, disgusted with the advice of his scout. He waved a hand and the column started forward again. In five minutes, they were wrapped in a cloud of dust caused by the horses. A choking cloud of dust that swirled around them, marking their line of march. Even with that marker, Custer believed that the Indians didn't know that they were close.

As they moved away from the Rosebud and into the valleys around the Little Bighorn, Brown moved up, closer to the general. When he was close, he said, "You realize the magnitude of the Indian village."

"Sir, I am not in the habit of taking my council from civilians, particularly civilians unschooled in military tactics or in the ways of the savages."

"Just thought I should mention it."

"The greater the number defeated, the greater the victory. I rejected soldiers from the Second so that the Seventh would get all the glory. Now I am not going to worry about the number of hostiles."

"I'm sure that there will be plenty of glory for the Seventh."

"You may rejoin your people," said Custer, dismissing him suddenly.

Brown rode off to the right where his people waited, just outside the cloud of dust.

"Well?"

Brown laughed. "The man is phenomenal. Does not believe that the Seventh can be defeated. I sat next to him while he refused to acknowledge the size of the Indian pony herd. Now, with his scouts telling him many men are going to die, he ignores his orders to rush toward the Sioux."

"So what do we do?" asked Thompson.

"We stand back and let history take its course. We stand back and wait for the decoy party and stop them before Custer can chase them."

She nodded. "I don't think I like this plan very much."

"Nothing not to like," said Brown, but he understood her reasoning. So much could go wrong so easily. There were too many people who had roles in the coming battle and none of the key players had seen the script, except for Brown and the people with him.

They rode on in silence, Brown trying to think of everything that could go wrong. Custer could take off after the Indians without a thought, they could hit from another area, they could be late or early or they could not show up, which was what Brown hoped for.

Custer increased the pace so that the column was moving at a fast trot. The noise being made was now magnified. The metal equipment rattled, the leather creaked and popped, and the horses were grunting with the effort. Custer didn't seem to notice that either.

About noon, Custer halted the column. They were near a shallow creek, the banks lined with trees and bushes. The water was splashing and bubbling. Custer dropped from his saddle and stood on the ground, looking back at the men of the Seventh as the column slowly closed the gaps and drew together. The dust drifted toward him, obscuring him momentarily. When it blew by him and he was visible again, he had moved. He was standing near the bugler, who blew officer's call once.

Brown took a deep breath and said, "This is it now. Custer is about to make the move to divide the regiment into three battalions. Pete, swing to the south. Jesse, you go with him. Andy, you'll be on the north with Munday. You see something, fire on it. Chase it away. If we can do that, then we'll have history back on course."

"Got it," said Baily. He grinned and hitchhiked a thumb over his shoulder. "Old George will be royally pissed if we fire, saying we alerted the Sioux."

"Pete, the Sioux know we're here. They'd have to be blind and stupid not to know. Look at that dust cloud we've created in our haste to get here. What Custer refuses to understand is that they don't care. All the medicine is on their side. They pushed Crook back and Sitting Bull has already had his vision. Soldiers falling into their village upside down. He knows that the soldiers will attack and they will be defeated."

"Where will you be?" asked Thompson.

"I'm going to listen to Custer. Make sure that we're on track. Now, let's do it."

As the people rode off to guard the head of the column, Brown walked toward the meeting of officers at Ash Creek. Again, Custer had his map out.

"Captain Benteen, you, with Companies D, H, and K, will swing to the south in search of the hostiles. That way you'll be in a position to block their route of retreat. Major Reno, you, with Companies A, G, and M, will follow the creek to the Little Bighorn and attack the end of the village. I'll take the remainder of the regiment, except Company B, to the north and support you with the whole regiment. Lieutenant McDugall, you will take Company B and remain with the pack train to guard it. Any questions?"

The men stood looking at the map and then at one another. They knew from long experience that Custer would not listen to anything anyone had to say. He was the commander and that was it. Orders were issued to be carried out and not to be questioned. Those who asked questions found himself on the outside. Now, with the enemy almost in sight, anyone questioning him would be considered a traitor.

"That's it then," said Custer. "Rejoin your units and prepare to move out."

As Custer turned to walk toward his horse, there was a burst of firing. Custer stopped and yelled, "Who's that shooting?"

Brown didn't have to ask. He knew because he had recognized the sound of the weapons. Baily and Thompson had just initiated the change they had been sent to make. They had found the decoys and were trying to stop them.

TWENTY-EIGHT

Hampton was too excited, too agitated, to eat breakfast, even though Jackson had made it. She sat in the chair, looked out the window, got out of the chair, and then walked around the table. She stood looking down at Jackson.

"Can't you hurry?"

Jackson took a big bite, chewed it slowly, and then swallowed. "Why? They won't arrive before ten in the morning and probably not until noon. No reason to hurry."

"But what if your logic is wrong?" asked Hampton. "What if they figure we'd be there early and then leave because we aren't there?"

"With time travel, they could make several checks a day in a matter of minutes," said Jackson, picking up the glass of juice. He drained it and added, "However, if you're that worried, we'll leave now."

"Finally," she said. She plucked her light suit jacket off the bed and put it on, moving directly to the door.

Jackson followed her and then made sure that the door was locked as they left. Again they hurried down the hall, waited for the elevator, and stepped down. The operator tried to get a conversation going. Hampton was too excited to talk and Jackson didn't feel like it.

On the street, there was a cold wind blowing. Icy. It tugged at their clothes and tried to steal their breaths. Newspaper tumbled by and when Hampton demanded he hurry, she created a small cloud of fog.

Hampton led the way, nearly dragging Jackson along Colfax, down the hill near the state capital, and out into the park. There weren't any bums left now. The cold had driven them into the city where they could find warm grates, a bus station, or a sheltered doorway to sleep in.

Hampton circled it once, searching for a sign that their rescue party had been there and gone. Jackson collapsed onto a bench, pulled his collar up, and hunched over, trying to shield himself from the cold. He studied the ground under his feet, a white coating of frost on it.

"Won't be here till noon," he said, not looking at her.

"And it won't hurt us to be here and wait," said Hampton.

He glanced at her, standing with her back to the sun, as if the feeble rays could warm her. She had her hands on her hips. Jackson shook his head and said, "Why is it that you have to do everything the hard way? Can't you listen just this once?"

"You don't know everything," she snapped.

"I know enough to stay out of the cold so that I don't freeze to death before we can get rescued."

"No," she said. "You just know enough to get us trapped here in 1950."

"Not my fault," said Jackson.

Before she could answer, there was a shimmering about twenty yards from them. It looked like a highway seen at high noon in the middle of the summer. A shifting of the light and a golden glow that appeared first as a ball of light. Jackson saw it before Hampton. He stared at it open-mouthed.

"I don't believe it," he said.

Hampton turned and saw and understood. "You don't know everything," she shouted.

The shape shimmered and shook and then solidified. The woman, dressed in an emerald jumpsuit that seemed to glow green, stepped forward.

"There is a problem?"

Jackson was on his feet. He recognized the woman immediately. "The retrieval bracelet was stolen, Pam. Now, get us out of here."

"Yes, sir." She glanced at Hampton and asked, "Did you complete the mission?"

Jackson shook his head. "We were jumped within an hour or two of arrival. Didn't get a chance."

"Then maybe we should . . ."

"Let's get out of here," said Hampton.

Jackson looked at Pam. "How is the other mission progressing?"

"Progress as of last night has been satisfactory."

"Good," said Jackson, grinning. "Let's get out of the open and head on home."

Hampton moved forward, a dozen questions in her mind. As she started to ask them, she realized that she hadn't been gone all that long. It wasn't as if a war were being fought. Everything should be the same as it was when they left.

Jackson headed toward a clump of trees. He stopped and asked, "You coming?"

Hampton joined him and then Pam came with them. They moved behind a bush that screened them from the streets that bordered the park. Jackson glanced upward, into the pale blue sky, the thin white clouds looking as if they had been brushed there with a tiny brush and only a little paint.

"Home," he said.

Pam looked at him, then Hampton, and touched the device on her wrist. "Home," she echoed.

The golden glow enclosed them, just as it did in the chamber. Jackson felt dizzy and light-headed as they started the trip into the future. He closed his eyes and crouched, taking a deep breath as they sped forward.

An instant later, there was a flash of light and then a brightness that wrapped them. Jackson opened his eyes and stood up. He glanced toward the control room, saw the lights there, and then moved toward the hatch.

"Made it," he said.

"Now all we have to do is see what changes have been made," said Hampton.

"None," said Pam. "None at all, according to the computer."

"Right," said Jackson.

TWENTY-NINE

Brown ran for his horse and leaped up into the saddle. Without waiting for anyone, he yanked on the reins, jerking the horse around. He spurred it on and took off, galloping up a slight ridge, to the south of the column, where the Indian village was hidden.

Custer and four of his officers were suddenly following him. Brown glanced back and saw them. The first company in line, Smith's Grey Horse Troop, had dismounted and were fanning out in a skirmish line, hurrying after them.

At the top of the rise, Brown could see all the way down, to the waters of the Little Bighorn. Baily and Thompson were about halfway down the slope, their horses tied behind them. They were crouched behind an outcropping of rock. A dozen Indians lay on the ground in front of them and another dozen or so were retreating rapidly.

Brown reined his horse to a halt and jumped off, grabbing at the rifle stuck in the scabbard. He knelt and aimed, firing at the farthest of the fleeing Sioux. He squeezed the trigger and felt the weapon kick. A moment later the Indian fell from his horse, rolled over, and didn't move.

Custer joined him. He sat there, the borrowed binoculars up to his eyes. "Stop them all," he ordered.

The other officers climbed from their horses and spread out. They began firing as both Baily and Thompson opened fire again. Another of the Indians fell, but they had reached the edge of the river.

Brown fired rapidly, pulling the trigger quickly. Another Sioux slipped from the saddle, falling on the bank close to the water. A fourth was hit and plunged into the Little Bighorn with a splash.

Suddenly the remaining Indians whirled, charging back up the hill.

"Kill them all," ordered Custer.

Brown lowered his weapon as the other officers fired. Two of the savages dropped, their horses continuing the attack riderless. The last of the Indians swerved, but it did them no good. A final volley cut them down.

With the threat suddenly gone, Baily and Thompson leaped from cover and ran to their horses. They climbed into the saddles and then rode back up the hill quickly.

"What in the hell were your people doing down there?" demanded Custer.

"Looking for the Indians."

"They've alerted the village now."

"No more than your campfires this morning or the dust from the column."

Custer looked at the officers and ordered, "Rejoin your troops now." He turned, saw that the skirmishers had nearly reached the hilltop, and waved at them, signaling them to return.

"Now, Mister Brown, I want to know what your people were doing on this side of the column."

"Looking for signs that the Indians were close."

"They seem to have found them."

Brown wanted to say something about hurrying, hoping that Custer wouldn't decide that it was time to change his mind. The regiment had to be divided. Rather than suggest anything, he said simply, "Yes, sir, they did."

As Baily and Thompson reached the top of the ridge, Custer turned his horse and started back toward the regiment. When he was out of earshot, Baily asked, "How we doing?"

"He isn't inclined to chase the decoys since we stopped them and he hasn't said a word about keeping the regiment together. I think we're okay."

As he spoke, Benteen and his three troops broke out of the formation and headed up the ridge. They came on slowly, reached the top, and started down, toward the bodies that lay on the grassy slope. Two men spurred forward and then halted, dropping to the ground. They looked at the dead men, then turned the bodies over so that they were facedown.

"Why do that?" asked Baily.

Thompson shrugged, but Brown said, "Cheyenne believe it's bad luck to leave the bodies of the enemy facing the sky. A little psychological warfare."

"Now what?" asked Thompson.

"I guess we rejoin Custer for a while, and then launch the recording device."

They headed down to the regiment. Reno and his men were separating themselves. They crossed the stream, and headed to the west, along Ash Creek. They dipped down, lost from sight, came up again, and then slipped away.

Custer was with the scouts when Brown, Baily, and Thompson joined them. Mitch Bouyer was there, again telling Custer that there were too many Indians now that the regiment had been divided.

"You talk like an old woman," said Custer. "If you want to go, go. Don't stay here if you're afraid."

"If we ride in there," said Bouyer, "we won't ride out again."

Custer took a deep breath and turned toward Bloody Knife. Using sign language, the Indian was saying to the sun, "I shall not see you go down behind the hills tonight."

Custer stared at him and said, "Go with Reno. Lead him to the east side of the village so that he can attack it."

As Bloody Knife rode off, Varnum and the other scouts joined him, riding after Reno. Only a few of them remained behind with Custer.

The general looked at Brown and asked, "What's your opinion of this?"

"You're the general," said Brown noncommittally.

"You don't think we're all going to die today?"

Brown shook his head and said, "I don't think so."

"Good, I want you and your people to remain with us."

Brown rubbed his face and said, "You think that's a good idea, General?"

"You scared like the rest of those cowards?"

"No, General."

"Then you can come with us. Help us find a ford so that we can hit the other end of the village. Catch them between two pinchers."

Now Brown hesitated. He stared at the general. His face seemed flushed with excitement. He looked at the others and then said, "I'll go down with you, but I think the rest of my people should be sent to join Benteen and Reno."

Custer rocked back in the saddle. "There a reason for this request?"

"I think that we could be more effective if we were spread out over the whole regiment."

"You can do what you want," said Custer. "I don't care, but I want you to ride down with me."

"Certainly," said Brown.

"Now wait a minute," said Thompson. "I'm not going to be detailed to run off to safety..."

"What do you mean safety?" asked Custer.

"It doesn't mean a thing," said Brown quietly. He looked at her. "You're not going with us."

"I am."

"And I," said Baily.

Brown looked at each of them. "You're sure about this?"

"If you're going with the general, then we're going too," said Thompson.

"You know what it means?"

"Not necessarily," said Thompson. "Forewarned is fore-armed."

"What are you all talking about," demanded Custer.

Brown looked him in the eye and said, "There are thousands of warriors down there and we're going to be riding into it without a thought."

"The Seventh Cavalry can handle any force of hostiles in the West," said Custer.

"I'm sure it can, General, but you're not riding in with the whole regiment. You've only five companies, less than half of it."

"Still a force that is sufficient to destroy the Indian village."

"Certainly," said Brown.

"What are you going to tell the others?" asked Thompson.

"I'll tell them to find Major Reno and stick with his command." He looked at her and then Baily. "We'll meet with them later."

Custer turned in the saddle, now ignoring the conversation. To the officers close to him, he said, "Let's get going."

They moved out then, along Ash Creek. They stopped to water the horses and as they did, Kent and Munday came riding up. Brown met them.

"You head on to join with Major Reno's battalion," he said.

Kent stared down at him. Everyone knew that Reno would hit the end of the village and be forced to flee. It wouldn't be an organized retreat, but a rout, with each man running for his life.

"You sure about that?"

Brown glanced right and left and said, "You know where Reno will end up. Go there and wait for the battalion. There won't be any Indians there until after the cavalry arrives."

"Where are you going to be?"

Again Brown looked around. "We're going to follow Custer for a while to answer a few of the questions. Once Martini leaves, we'll break away too."

"Martini?"

"Custer will send him out with a message for Benteen. We'll get out then."

"You sure?"

"Of course," said Brown. "I have no desire to commit suicide with the Seventh."

"All right," said Kent.

Sturgis then broke from formation, riding toward them. He stopped short and said, "The general has ordered me to ride with you from this moment on."

"He still doesn't trust us."

"No, sir," said Sturgis, "I don't think it's that. I think he wants me here to act as a liaison. Told me to tell you that you're to report any of your impressions as you get them."

Kent took a deep breath and said, "Maybe we'd better stay with you, rather than getting us scattered all over the countryside."

"No," said Brown. He looked pointedly at Munday and then down at her wrist. "There are chances that we don't want to take."

"I understand," said Kent.

Brown pulled out his pocketwatch. "I make it three, three and a half hours until we'll be back here. Then, depending on the situation, we can see about heading out again."

"The place is going to be thick with hostiles," said Sturgis. "We're going to be stirring them up so that they'll be madder than hornets."

"No matter," said Brown. "They'll be here and we'll be riding to the east."

Custer shouted an order and the first of the seven companies with him moved out. It looked to be Company F, commanded by Yates. Custer was in front of them with a small group of scouts and a couple of the officers.

"Lieutenant, there they go."

"Yes, sir. We'd better get moving."

Brown looked at Kent and Munday. "You two have your instructions."

"I don't like them," said Kent.

"But you'll obey them."

Kent nodded and said, "Of course." He turned to Munday. "Ready."

"Let's go."

Kent hesitated. "You sure," he asked Brown again.

"Yes. You've got to protect the recall bracelet."

Kent was surprised that Brown would say anything about it in front of Sturgis, but then remembered that Sturgis wouldn't survive the battle. It didn't matter.

"Good luck," he said. Without another word he spurred his horse forward. Munday followed closely. They turned and followed the path that Reno had used.

As they disappeared, Brown looked at the people with him. "This is it then."

Sturgis looked from one face to another and said, "You people act as if we are riding to our doom."

"You think about it, Lieutenant," said Brown. "You watched the scouts sing their death songs and you heard the warnings given to the general."

"Sure, but those are heathens who don't understand modern warfare."

"Just thought you should know what we're about to ride into," said Brown.

"We'll survive," said Sturgis. "Hell, we'll win."

"It's hard to beat a man with that attitude," said Brown. He looked at his people and said, "If you're ready, let's do it."

"I'll never be ready," said Thompson, "but let's do it anyway."

With that they spurred their horses and fell in behind the Grey Horse Troop.

THIRTY

It took Kent and Munday almost thirty minutes to catch up to the rear of Reno's battalion. The soldiers were no longer trying to remain silent and they weren't worried about their trail. They were throwing away the things they thought would hinder them in the upcoming fight. They wanted their rifles, pistols, and ammo. Little else mattered.

They came to a ford, crossed the South Fork, then re-crossed Ash Creek. Kent found where the soldiers had crossed it, but this time he and Munday didn't follow. Instead, they stayed on the north side of the Little Bighorn, moving toward the bluffs where Reno would come after his failure to drive into the Indian village.

They crossed some open ground, worked their way around a thick stand of trees, and then climbed up the back side of the bluff. They came to the top, where there was a slight depression. The south side of it dropped away sharply, down toward the Little Bighorn. Across the river were more trees and to the west they could see the edge of the Indian village, a mass of teepees that lined the bank as far as they could see.

Kent stopped his horse and got off. He pulled his rifle out and moved to the south edge of the bluff, crouching down. He could see a cloud of dust on the southwest side of the Little Bighorn. To the northeast was a second, which had to be Custer and his five companies.

"Now what?" asked Munday.

"I guess we wait. We're set here and there's no reason for us to move."

But he didn't sit there. Instead, he circled the top of the bluff, checking the approaches to it and examining the fields of fire. He put his training from the Army and a tour in Vietnam into play. He returned to where Munday crouched.

"They'll be coming from that direction when they come," said Kent.

"And we . . . ?"

"Cover them as best we can, but Reno and the majority of his command will reach the top here without our help."

"From over there?" she asked.

Kent shrugged. "I don't know the exact sequence of events. Reno and his men will hit the village, be driven out, form a second skirmish line, and then retreat across the river."

"When?"

Kent stood up and looked to the west. He could see the dust from Reno's column though the men were hidden behind the trees. He moved to the very edge of the bluff and looked down the steep slopes, surprised that horses and men would be able to climb it, but knew they would.

As he turned to look back at Munday, he heard the first of the firing. "Be about an hour," said Kent.

"God," said Munday, "I don't like the way this is going."

"Neither do I," said Kent, "but there is nothing we can do about it."

Reno and the three companies that made up his battalion hesitated at the Little Bighorn, and then carefully forded it. He formed them on the south side of the river. The lay of the land and the trees blocked his view of the Indian village. He pulled his pistol and waved a hand, motioning the battalion forward.

They moved off, forming on line so that all the hundred and fifty soldiers were riding directly at the target. They entered the trees, rode through the forest, and came out onto open ground. They crossed a wide, shallow ravine and came up, looking at the village. For an instant, it looked peaceful enough. No sign that the Sioux there suspected an attack was coming.

Then, almost as if an alarm had been raised, warriors came boiling out of the village. First a dozen, then fifty, and then a hundred of them rode toward the soldiers, screaming and firing rifles and pistols.

Reno held up a hand, halting the halfhearted advance. The men with him, spread out on either side of him, stopped too. Horses pawed the ground and the men nervously studied the onrushing Sioux.

From a shallow ravine ahead and to the left, Reno thought he saw more hostiles waiting for him. The warriors who had attacked now whirled and retreated, fleeing toward the village. Reno waved his battalion forward again, chasing the Sioux, but then, fearing a trap, he slowed the assault.

Unsure of what to do, and seeing no sign that Custer had launched his attack at the far end, Reno halted his command. As firing broke out, rippling along his line, and the Sioux came forward again, he leaped from his saddle.

"Dismount! Fight on foot!"

The three companies with him spread out, the men moving forward to the line. A fifth of the soldiers remained in the rear, holding the reins of the battalion's horses. There was a rattling, as the men began to fire again, but it wasn't a coordinated volley.

One private's horse suddenly bolted, the man still in the saddle. He leaned forward, hanging on as the frightened animal raced toward the Indians.

Reno, a pistol in his hand, ordered, "Take the horses to the trees." He then crouched, watched the hostiles momentarily, and then fired at them.

The men continued to move until they had a thin skirmish line formed. One end was anchored in the trees, near where the horses were now hidden. The other was floating free, a hundred and fifty yards away.

The men were firing wildly now, though the Sioux were still hundreds of yards away. There was a little return fire, though some of the Indians were riding to attack the soldiers with war clubs and rifle butts.

There never was a coordinated attack from the village. As the warriors grabbed their weapons, they leaped on their horses and charged into the battle, shooting as they did.

Reno turned to Bloody Knife. "What are they going to do? I have to know."

"Indians attack," he said, telling the major nothing he didn't already know.

"How? Where?"

The scout was staring at the major when his face seemed to explode. Blood, brains, and bone were blown out, splattering Reno. For a moment, the major was stunned, unable to move. Bloody Knife dropped, dead before he hit the ground.

The firing around them grew heavier. Now the Indians, as many as a thousand, were coming at them. Screaming savages, waving their weapons. Soldiers were dropping and a few had turned to run. Another horse bolted, the rider unable to stop it or turn it. The Sioux caught him and dragged him from the saddle, beating him and stabbing him.

Reno glanced along his line. The Sioux were attacking the left side of it and had overrun part of it, getting behind the soldiers. Men were caught in a cross fire. More men were falling. A few were running, frightened. There were shouts from the soldiers. Cries of fear and desperation. The firing rose in volume and then dropped off as the soldiers tried to reload before the Sioux could get to them.

Suddenly the ambush that had caught him and killed twenty of his men in thirty seconds during the Civil War flashed before him. A trap that had been sprung with deadly efficiency just as this one was being sprung. Reno saw it all again. A thousand Sioux riding at him, screaming. His men were dying a little too rapidly. The open ground in front of the trees was turning into a death trap.

"Fall back," he ordered suddenly. He had envisioned, briefly, an orderly retreat. "Fall back."

But it wasn't a retreat. It was a scramble for safety with those closest to him whirling and running, leaving behind those who hadn't heard the order, fighting for their lives.

All around him, the defense broke down. Soldiers hearing Reno's order turned and ran for the trees. And Reno didn't want to be left alone. He followed them, running along with them. Some turned and fired, others just ran.

Those who didn't hear the order saw the first group deserting them and took off after them. The defense collapsed completely and the Sioux swarmed forward. They chased down the soldiers, clubbing them to the ground. They shot at them with bows and arrows and rifles. More of the soldiers died. Some of them screamed for help that never came. Others tried to fight their way clear.

Most of the soldiers who reached the trees turned to fight again. Using the available cover, they attempted to stop the Indian assault. Again they were fighting, firing at the Sioux who were mopping up the stragglers.

"We're cut off, sir," yelled a sergeant over the rising noise of the battle.

Reno glared at him. "I know that."

"Where's the general?" he demanded. "I thought he was going to support us."

"Will you shut up?" snapped Reno. He wanted silence so that he could concentrate. He wanted everyone to be quiet. But the screaming Sioux and the firing wouldn't be silenced. The Sioux kept up the pressure.

His men were still shooting, trying to maintain their position and organize a defense. The Indians were staying away from the woods, riding close and darting away. They were counting coup.

More Indians were pouring out of the village. Reinforcements for the Sioux. The firing increased as the Indians probed closer and closer, almost daring the soldiers to shoot at them and kill them.

"We've got to get clear," shouted a lieutenant.

"We've got to stay," countered Reno. "The general will relieve us."

"Where is he?"

Reno turned and looked at the man. And then turned to face the oncoming Sioux. He raised his pistol, standing sideways like a man in a duel. He aimed and carefully pulled the trigger. His weapon was empty.

Around him the men were wild. They were trying to find protection. They were shouting. They were screaming. They were shooting and not reloading. A sergeant ran along the line trying to get the troopers to fire. Trying to get them to put out rounds and halt the Indian counterattack.

Another soldier fired once and then threw down his rifle. He clawed at his holster, trying to get his pistol free. A bullet struck him in the shoulder, spinning him. He fell, rolled, and got to his knees. He held out his hands, almost as if he were praying, and then fell forward, on his face.

For a moment the fight stabilized. The soldiers were firing rapidly, the smoke from their weapons filling the air like a thick fog rolling in from the ocean. All around there was a cacophony of sound. Horses screaming in terror. Men shouting orders. Bugles. Screams of pain and horror. Firing. Indians attacking, whooping.

Reno reloaded and emptied his pistol and then looked down at it as if it had betrayed him in some fashion. He seemed unconcerned with the rapid disintegration of his command. There was nothing around him that interested him.

Then, suddenly, the woods was filled with Indians. They had raced across the open ground and were among the cavalry. Screaming and whooping. They set fire to the grass at one end of the valley so that the smoke mixed with the burnt powder, turning the sun a dull red and hiding friend from the enemy. The defense began to fall apart.

Using the smoke for cover, the Indians moved closer still. They would pop up, fire, and then drop, moving through the trees. Some were behind Reno and his men. All around men were shooting as fast as they could, but there was no fire discipline. It was just men shooting to be shooting with no thought to coordination with the rest of the command.

Reno decided he could take no more. His battalion was falling apart. He whirled, ran to the rear, and leaped to the saddle of the nearest horse. "Let's go," he shouted as he tried to reach the river.

An officer yelled after him, then spun and ordered, "Men! To your horses!"

A scout demanded, "What damn fool move is this?"

Suddenly the firing dropped off as the soldiers tried to get away. One man's horse bolted, dragging him toward a party of Sioux. Others got into the saddle and wheeled, riding for the river, Reno in the lead.

There was no thought of the wounded. Those who couldn't get to their horses or get themselves out of the trees were left behind.

Reno rode along the riverbank, searching for a way to get down it. Finally, a mile from where the second line had collapsed, he forced his horse to jump into the water. It struggled across the cold waters of the Little Bighorn as what was left of the battalion followed.

Reno's adjutant, Lieutenant Benjamin Hodgson, was hit in the knee, the bullet killing his horse just as he reached the riverbank. He was pitched into the water and struggled to the surface. A trooper thrust a stirrup at him and he was dragged across the river to the other side.

Reynolds, who had told Custer that the valley was alive with Indians, didn't make it to the river. His horse was shot once. It fell, trapping him by pinning one of his legs. Reynolds tried to push himself free. He braced a foot on the saddle and shoved, but the dead horse weighed too much. There was nothing for him to do but fight where he was. He used his rifle, firing rapidly, but there were too many Indians. He died in a hail of bullets and arrows.

Now most of the soldiers who still lived had made it to the Little Bighorn. With the Sioux chasing them, they didn't slow. Some of the soldiers who lost their horses tried to find cover in the valley. The Sioux, chasing the soldiers to the river, rode past them, ignoring them. A lucky few escaped that way.

The battle was suddenly on the riverbanks. Some of the Indians were on the north side, shooting down at the soldiers as they tried to get out of the water. The water was boiling, blood floating in it, turning it crimson.

Hodgson, having reached the north bank, turned the stirrup loose and tried to scramble up the muddy, slippery bank. Another bullet struck him, throwing him back down into the water, dead.

Men were scrambling out of the water. The firing was going on around them. Men were still falling. One Sioux darted in, touched a wounded cavalryman to count coup, and then tried to flee. A soldier shot him in the back. The savage slipped from his horse and into the water.

Now the men were struggling up the bluffs to the top. The Sioux chased them, dragging a few of the stragglers from their horses and killing them quickly. A soldier kicked his way free of them and then fell from his horse. He rolled to his back and shot one Sioux. Then he died as the Indians rode over him.

At the top of the bluff, Kent listened and watched. As Reno's men hit the village, he could see movement. Shapes, but not individuals. He could hear the firing and then the shouting as the battle was joined. As the men retreated, he saw the smoke billow as the two sides fired at one another. That was partially obscured as the Indians set the grass on fire.

When the retreat across the river started, Kent was ready. Lying on his stomach, he used his rifle to fire into the Indian positions.

He saw Hodgson hit and fall into the river. He saw him dragged out and then hit a second time. As that happened, he spotted an Indian pulling on the scalp of a wounded soldier. Kent aimed at him and fired. The Sioux pitched into the water, but a second took the place of the first.

Now the soldiers were halfway up the slopes. The Indians were falling away, letting the soldiers go. The firing slowed as the first of the cavalrymen reached the top of the bluff. For a moment they caught their breaths and then whirled, firing down at the savages.

But it was too late. The Indians were fleeing. They were attacking back across the river, riding away rapidly. One of the officers was trying to organize a makeshift defense.

The doctor crawled close to the major. "What in the hell was that?"

"That was a cavalry charge, sir!"

THIRTY-ONE

As soon as the hatch was opened, Jackson was out of the shoot chamber, running down the hall to the stairs. He didn't wait for Hampton, or the two technicians who wanted to ask him questions. Instead, he ran to the stairs, up them, and then down the hall into the conference room. Inside, he stopped long enough to glance first at the two men and one woman working there, and then up at the board that still showed a map of Denver in 1950.

Jackson moved forward rapidly, opened the door, and ordered, "Give me the Little Bighorn in June, 1876."

The supervisor glanced back and asked, "Are your taking over?"

Jackson stepped to the chair and said, "Yes. Yes." As the man got out of the way, Jackson took his place. To the female technician he said, "Give me the Little Bighorn."

Hampton caught up with him then and stood behind him. "What's happening?"

The map came up on the big board. The streets of Denver faded, replaced by the plains of Montana with the Little Bighorn shown in the center.

Hampton pointed up at it. "They've moved beyond the critical point."

Jackson rocked back in the chair and suddenly relaxed. He stared up at the map and said, "Then the change has been initiated."

"That would seem to be indicated," agreed Hampton, her voice calm.

"Have they asked for recall?"

The technician shook his head. "Nothing." He pointed and added, "Given the information, it seems that they're up on Reno Hill. They've already hit the eastern side of the

Indian village. Do you want to pull them out now?"

Jackson turned to Hampton and then said, "No. Not until they've asked for it."

"And if they're unable?" asked Hampton, thinking of their own problem.

"All indications are that they've reached safety on Reno Hill."

"Except the Sioux will be sniping at it all night and through most of the next day. They're still in danger."

Jackson turned and studied the map. There was no way to be sure what was happening in the battle, except that it seemed that his team had moved to the bluffs on the northern side of the river. According to the history, about the time Reno reached that point, Custer was attacking the other end of the village.

"Which means that our people need to stay only another hour or so to get the pictures we want," he said quietly.

"And then we retrieve them."

"No, not until they ask for it," said Jackson.

"Have you forgotten what happened to us already?" she asked him.

"No, but if they've gotten separated, a retrieval now would only complicate the problem."

"So we wait?"

"We wait," said Jackson. To himself, he thought, We wait until I see something that suggests they need help. He kept his eyes on the map.

THIRTY-TWO

The activity on the plateau above the Little Bighorn was furious. Men were scrambling around, throwing down equipment, boxes, saddles, and scrapping frantically at the sun-baked soil, trying to erect barricades for protection. Around them horses were screaming in terror. Indians were howling and hooting, firing at the top of the bluff, trying to kill the hundred men who had survived the aborted attack against the Sioux village and Reno's cavalry charge.

Kent crouched near the edge of the bluff and watched as warriors worked the field and the riverbanks, searching for wounded men, killing them, and mutilating the bodies of those already dead. Others kept the pressure on the soldiers, dancing around the cover, popping up and firing with rifles and bows and arrows before diving back down.

Reno stood behind a horse, a silver flask in his hand. He drank deeply, ignoring the cries of the wounded around him. Orders were being shouted as the company commanders and NCOs tried to organize a defense. The troopers knew what had to be done and tried to do it. With knives, canteen cups, and bare hands, they were scraping at the earth, trying to dig firing pits.

Munday crawled to Kent and tried to see down into the Little Bighorn Valley. In the distance, to the west, she could see the shallow waters sparkling as the river wormed its way through the valley.

Looking at her, Kent said, "Another hour, maybe two, and we can get out of here."

"You think Brown and the others will get back?"

Kent shrugged. "I think that Brown knows exactly what is going on and will make a move to get himself and the others away from Custer."

157

"And then we punch out?"

"Exactly."

Then, suddenly, the pressure from the Sioux and Cheyenne evaporated completely. The Indians turned and fled back across the Little Bighorn, running up the southern bank.

"What the hell?" asked Munday.

Kent understood it, but couldn't say anything about it. Not with a hundred soldiers, the majority of whom would survive the fight now that they had reached the bluff, close enough to overhear.

As the shooting tapered and then stopped, the exhausted, frightened men slumped to the ground. They lay there, forgetting about the Indians for the moment. Then, slowly, one by one, they began to move again, working to strengthen the breastworks and barricades, throwing down anything they thought would turn a bullet, preparing for the next assault. They all knew it would come because the Indians never gave up when they smelled a victory. At the moment, those three companies of the Seventh were ripe for plucking. Even a halfhearted attack would have overrun them.

But there was one hope for them. It was on the lips of most as they claimed that Custer would save them. Custer and the rest of the regiment would be their salvation.

Others, however, weren't so optimistic. They were cussing the general, claiming that he had deserted them. He had tried to sacrifice them, and they'd get even later. Those were the men who remembered Major Elliott at the Washita.

But now that they were momentarily safe on the bluff, the men were asking each other, "Where is Custer? Where is the general?"

Custer pushed his five companies of the Seventh hard once the column had been split up. After four days of almost constant movement, both the men and the animals were beginning to show the strain. Several troopers were on foot, leading their exhausted animals.

They moved along the northern side of the river, using

the lay of the land to conceal themselves from the Indians. After only a few minutes of rapid travel, Custer halted them because he could see, in the distance, the Indian encampment. On the far side of the river, on open ground that stretched nearly to the horizon, were thousands of teepees. Custer, rather than worry about the size of the village, was suddenly elated. There had been no attempt to break the camp and he interpreted that as meaning they had caught the Indians napping. As soon as they attacked, the surprise would be complete.

Turning in the saddle, he shouted, "We've got them, boys. We've got them this time."

Without further comment, Custer waved them on, riding hard. At the head of the Medicine Tail Coulee, he stopped them again. He glanced to the right, where his enlisted aide for the day rode, and said, "Martini, I want you to find Captain Benteen. Tell him we've found a big village. Tell him to hurry and tell him to bring the packs. You understand?"

Before he could answer, Cooke, the adjutant, scribbled a note with the instructions on it. "You give this to Captain Benteen. You understand?"

"Yes," said Martini.

"Then go," said Custer. "And hurry."

Martini wheeled his horse and began to ride off at a fast trot.

Thompson, who was now very close to Brown, asked, "That the last man to see Custer?"

"Yes."

"Maybe it's time for us to get out of here," she said.

"We've got a few minutes. Custer is going to hesitate here briefly."

The scouts with him were off their horses. They moved away from the column and crouched, each singing his death song. Custer watched the ritual quietly, as he had several times in the last few days.

"You men afraid?" he shouted at them. "Worried about the savages opposite us? You've done your jobs. Go ahead. Run away now."

Turning away from the scouts, Custer looked to the

right, at Brown and his little party. "You people can leave too."

Sturgis, who had been hanging in the rear of Brown's group, started to turn.

"That is, if you're afraid," said Custer.

Brown stared at the shining blue eyes and the ruddy face that was now flushed with excitement. He knew exactly what was going to happen. There was an obligation of one soldier to another. He should tell Custer that there would be thousands of Sioux, Cheyenne, and Arapahoe to oppose his two hundred soldiers. Without repeating rifles and without a defensible position, they would stand no chance.

But there was also an obligation to history. Custer had to ride into the valley and lose. That was the way history had been written.

"We're not afraid," said Brown evenly.

"Then stick close to me."

"Of course," said Brown.

As the scouts returned to their horses, Custer said, "Then we'll destroy the enemy now."

"Your orders?" said Brown quietly.

"I'm not going to allow those savages to escape. Orders are designed to be superseded, and I've just found ample cause to ignore them."

Brown grinned at that. If Custer succeeded, no one would even remember that he had been told to wait, and if he failed, he would be dead and therefore beyond the punishment of boards of inquiry.

He turned and saw Martini at the top of the ridge. The lone man stopped, looked at the column, and then rode out of sight. As he disappeared, Thompson said, "When are we going to get out of here?"

"After the attack begins," said Brown as he looked beyond her toward Sturgis.

The lieutenant moved forward, breaking into the conversation. "Stay close to me."

"No, Lieutenant," said Brown. "You stay close to us. Stick to us like glue."

With a single whoop, Custer waved the column forward. They swept down the coulee toward the river. There was firing in the front as the first contact was made. Indians, hiding in the grass near the bank of the Little Bighorn, fired a few random shots and then turned to flee.

In that moment, Custer was sure that he had won. The Indians, caught by surprise, would not be able to mount a defense before the soldiers rode into the center of the camp. Then they'd have to protect their families.

A hundred yards from the river, the situation changed. Indians seemed to rise from the ground. Those who had been fleeing stopped, leaped from their horses, and opened fire. Then, from the river hundreds more appeared, screaming and firing and waving blankets to frighten the cavalry mounts.

The assault petered out and then halted almost as if Custer had ordered it. Custer sat on his horse looking confused. More Sioux came from the east, firing rifles and using their bows. Several soldiers tumbled from their saddles and several men in the rear broke, galloping for the safety of the ridgeline behind them.

Custer, a pistol in his hand, studied the situation. He glanced right and left.

"General," yelled Yates, "we've got to move."

"To the right," shouted someone.

"Up the hill. Take the high ground."

The air was thick with gunsmoke and dust kicked up by the horses. Men were shouting. Two more fell. One tried to climb up, onto his horse, the blood staining his blue coat. His right arm hung down, useless.

"General, we're getting cut to pieces," announced one of the officers.

Custer shook himself, as if coming out of a trance. Wildly he looked around, seeing the Sioux boiling out of the village, the Cheyenne attacking from the left and the Arapahoe right in front. Hundreds of Indians, fighting to keep the soldiers away from their village.

Custer sprang into action. "Yates, wheel and assault to the right. Carry it to the top of the ridge and hold your ground there." Glancing to the rear, he shouted, "Lieutenant Calhoun, deploy your men for a defensive action. Hold here and then follow us."

Calhoun nodded and shouted, "Yes, sir."

"Bugler, sound the charge."

"Sir?"

"Sound the charge!" Custer wheeled his horse and faced to the west, toward the open plain that swept upward until it dominated the surrounding countryside. He spurred his horse and did the one thing that had worked for him all during the Civil War. He attacked blindly, believing that his men would follow him anywhere.

"Charge," he ordered. And rode for the top of the ridge to the west. The column turned with him and did as he commanded. They attempted to take the high ground.

They failed.

THIRTY-THREE

The attack up the hillside appeared to work. For a moment. Calhoun's company kept the Sioux and Cheyenne from following as the rest of the regiment seemed to break free of the Indians. Custer, at the front, spurred his horse on, racing for the high ground. Then, just before they could gain the crest, a huge party of Indians appeared, swarming over the top like ants attacking a picnic.

Almost without thinking, Custer turned again, heading down the hill, toward the river, but that was blocked too. Thousands of Indians. Suddenly there were Sioux and Cheyenne all around him. Thousands of the hostiles riding among the troops, trying to count coup. The hills were alive with them, surrounding Custer's five companies easily.

Custer slid to a halt. He saw the Grey Horse Troop close to him. "Lieutenant Smith, deploy to the east. Cover our flank."

Smith nodded and turned. He waved at his men and then attacked down the slope, toward the river. For some reason, Boston Custer and Henry Reed went with him, leaving the general above them.

"Tom, deploy down the slope to cover the flank there."

"Sure thing."

Custer watched the Indians rushing toward them. More of his men were dying, falling from the saddles. Horses were rearing in fright, making it impossible to coordinate the fire.

"Fight on foot," he ordered. "Dismount."

Those closest to him heard the order and obeyed it. A few of the men shot their horses, using the bodies as makeshift barricades, crouching behind them.

Miles Keogh and I Company were deployed to the east, near the top of the ridge to support both Yates and Smith. They fired down into the Indian attack.

Brown turned in his saddle as a sergeant jammed Custer's guidon into the ground, and grabbed the miniature camera that he had been given so long ago. He touched the button at the top and opened his hand as it began to spin away, launching itself into the sky. In an instant it was invisible to the men on the field. Just a speck that was recording the battle.

As he launched it, he turned to Sturgis. "It's time to get out."

"We can't leave."

"Lieutenant, if we stay, we're all going to die. We have got to get out now, while we can."

"No!"

Before Brown could argue further, there was a wet slap. A bullet striking flesh. The color drained from Brown's face and he swayed to the side. He opened his mouth to say something and then dropped to the ground.

Thompson leaped from the saddle. She knelt next to him and touched his throat. "NO!" she screamed. "NO!"

Baily didn't hesitate. "Jessie. We've got to get out now." He spun on Sturgis. "You have to assist us."

Sturgis was staring at the body of Brown. His blood soaked the dried grass near his side. His face was pale, looking waxy. His eyes were open, staring up into the late afternoon sun, glazing over.

"No!" yelled Thompson, forgetting everything she had ever learned.

Baily leaned over and grabbed at her shoulder. "Snap out of it."

She wasn't interested in snapping out of it or in what Baily had to say. She jerked her weapon from the scabbard on the saddle and knelt over Brown's body. She sighted and fired, aimed again and fired again.

Baily leaped from his horse, dropping next to her. "We don't get out, we'll die too."

"I don't care."

"Won't do any good to sacrifice yourself."

She kept firing at everything that moved, pulling the trigger again and again until the weapon was empty. She threw it down and clawed at her side, trying to draw her pistol.

Custer had stabilized the fight. The men were putting out rounds, firing into the mass of Indians that were darting around them like mosquitoes after a feast. In and out. Strike and retreat.

Smith's Grey Horse Troop was being pushed back though, giving ground until they found a deep ravine. At first it seemed to be the natural place to take cover, but then it turned into a death trap. The soldiers, lining the sides of the ravine, stretching out, were firing at the Indians who took cover behind bushes, rocks, and in other ravines. But the savages refused to show themselves. Instead, they fired the arrows upward, letting them arc to the ground into the circle of Smith's men, striking them in the backs.

One by one, the soldiers died until the force was too small to withstand an assault. The Sioux attacked then, running at them with clubs and knives, leaping among them slashing and hitting. The fight became hand to hand. Smith's men were overwhelmed and killed quickly. Smith, himself, maybe trying to save Custer's youngest brother and his nephew, escaped the destruction of his company. He scrambled clear. The two civilians died with the men of E Company, but Smith ran up the hill to join Custer and the remains of the battalion.

To the east, Calhoun and L Company were in serious trouble. The Sioux were working to annihilate it. They were dancing around it, flitting in and out, striking, killing, and running. They stampeded the horses away from the cavalrymen and then chased down the bigger mounts.

Custer, along with Yates and F Company, had secured their position for the moment. They watched L Company fight for its life. For an instant it looked as if Custer was going to order a rescue but then the Indians swarmed forward as they had done with E Company. They overran the position, clubbing the wounded and shooting everyone around them. In seconds it was over. Calhoun and two of his sergeants tried to join Keogh's I Company, but they were caught and killed.

Custer watched the death of L Company with a look of horror on his face. Maybe it was because he saw his brother-in-law Calhoun killed. Maybe it was the mutilation of the dead that shocked him. He'd seen the results before, but never had he witnessed the Indians slashing at the bodies of the newly dead.

Now Custer crouched near his personal guidon, his pistol on the ground near his knee. He scribbled a note on a sheet of paper pulled from his pocket. As the Indians whooped and hollered and continued to fire, he forced the message into the hand of a young lieutenant near him. Over the sound of the battle, he screamed, "You get this to Benteen. Not Reno, but Benteen. We'll hold here."

"No, sir. I won't abandon the fight."

"You'll do as ordered."

Baily, standing near, leaped forward. "I'll take it," he said.

Custer looked up at him and nodded. "Benteen. You get it to Benteen."

"Me and Thompson and Sturgis," said Baily.

"Go! Now!"

Thompson looked at the body of Brown. He'd been hit again by an arrow. It pierced his skull, pinning it to the ground. Fresh blood flowed from the wound.

"Jessie, let's go."

Now she didn't resist him. He helped her up into the saddle and as he did, he was hit. The round punched into his side, driving him forward. He grunted in surprise and pain, and slipped to one knee.

"Pete?"

"I'm fine. Let's go," he said.

Sturgis was on his horse, crouched low, hugging the animal's neck. Now with the gunsmoke thick on the hillside, it was hard to see anything and harder to breathe. The acrid smoke stung the mouth, nose, and lungs. Baily coughed once and then spasmodically, doubling over.

"Get out of here," shouted Custer.

Baily tried to mount and as he did, a brave ran at him, leaping to his back, forcing him to the ground. Thompson whirled, her horse rearing as she fired down. She missed. The Indian raised his knife and seized a handful of Baily's hair. Before he could slash at it, Thompson fired again and the Sioux died.

Slowly Baily stood up. Blood soaked his side. He was leaning over, a hand against the cloth, now stained crimson. "Get out," he said hoarsely.

Thompson shook her head, but as she did, she spurred her horse. It leaped forward. Sturgis joined her, riding toward the top of the ridge.

Around them the Indians shouted. Bullets and arrows snapped past them. Thompson, like Sturgis, leaned low, holding onto the horse's neck. Several Indians, fearing that soldiers were going to escape the trap, gave chase.

As they fled, Sturgis slipped to the rear. He fired at the pursuing braves, but that didn't stop them. They came on, shouting, screaming, and firing the captured rifles.

They reached the top of the ridge and below them was nothing. No Indians, no soldiers, just open ground that led away from the fight. Thompson turned toward the east, running toward the bluffs where Reno would be waiting, and where Benteen would arrive in minutes.

She glanced over her shoulder and saw that they were leaving the Indians behind. All the accounts of the massacre she'd ever read said that no one who rode in with Custer got out, but she was about to make it. The Indians would never catch her.

Suddenly there was a burning in her back, high, almost between her shoulder blades. A fiery sting that spread pain through her chest, making it hard to breathe. A white-hot fire poking through her. She sat straight up, unaware of what she was doing, and tumbled over the rear of the horse. Pain exploded in her back and she momentarily lost consciousness.

An instant later, Sturgis was kneeling near her, one hand outstretched as he aimed with his pistol. Only two of the Indians were riding toward them now, the others having given up to return to the battle. Sturgis fired and one of them dropped from the saddle. Carefully he aimed and fired. The second died then.

Now they were alone on the reverse side of the hill, a mile or more from the battle. The firing was heavy and the sky above them was full of smoke and dust. The sun was a fiery orange orb over them.

"We're clear," said Sturgis quietly.

"Makes no difference," she said. She coughed once, blood spraying from her mouth. She closed her eyes and seemed to collapse inward as she died.

Sturgis knelt there for a moment, holding her, listening to the fight. Now he didn't know what to do. The message he was carrying would come too late and there was no reason to return to Custer. One more gun wasn't going to help him.

Sturgis gently lowered Thompson to the ground and climbed slowly on his horse. His regiment was being wiped out and he wasn't there with it. Another man might have tried to reach Benteen, give him the note, and then make a grandstand play about returning. Another man might have ridden back over the hill to face death with his fellows.

Sturgis elected neither of those courses. Instead, he reined his horse around and rode off, toward the north, putting distance between himself and the massacre.

Back on the other side of the hill, Custer's men were dying faster and faster. Yates, Tom Custer, Cooke, and Smith were gathered around the general's guidon. They had assembled for the final instructions. The troops were arranged around them in a makeshift quickly shrinking battalion, fighting for their very lives.

"We've got to establish a defense," shouted Yates.

"Have everyone still alive fall back to here," ordered Custer.

"And then?" asked Tom.

"We'll try to break out, scatter, and rejoin Benteen and Reno. It's the only hope now."

The circle around them was getting smaller. The Indians

were diving in and out of the lines now, shrieking. Firing was still heavy.

As they watched, a soldier leaped to the back of one of the few horses still remaining with the cavalry. He fired at a Sioux warrior who ran at him and then spurred the animal. It jumped once, reared back, frightened, and then bolted up the hill. Cheyenne Indians ran after the man, but failed to catch him. He fired at them and then threw away his pistol. At the top of the hill, a savage stood holding a rifle. He aimed carefully and shot the soldier out of the saddle. When the man fell, the Indian ran forward, grabbed at his hair, and began hacking at it, trying to cut it off.

"Gentlemen," said Custer, suddenly calm. His whole demeanor had changed abruptly. He crouched near his guidon. "Let's get the men formed here. We'll live or die on this ground."

"Yes, sir," said Tom. He turned and seemed to step into a bullet. He fell to his side and struggled to sit up.

Directly to the east, Miles Keogh still sat on his horse. He was trying to rally his rapidly shrinking command. He shouted orders, pointed at the enemy, and tried to establish fields of fire, but his command was disintegrating too quickly. The men were giving up rapidly. One soldier stood, holding his rifle in front of him like it was an offering to a god. A Sioux warrior ran at him, took the rifle away, and killed him with his own weapon.

"Come on, boys," yelled Keogh. "Hold on. Make your shots count."

There was a sudden stinging at his knee. Pain flashed up his leg. For an instant he thought he was going to be sick. Instead, he clamped his teeth.

Leaning forward, he forced his horse, Comanche, to kneel. The animal followed Keogh's instructions and the officer slipped from the saddle. Wrapping the reins around his hand, he sat on the ground, still shouting at his men, trying to get them to fight harder.

A second round caught him in the chest. He grunted and said quietly, "Oh." Slowly he fell back, still holding onto the reins of his horse.

Those men of I Company who still lived abandoned

their positions then. They fled to the rear, toward Custer and the last of the battalion.

Custer knelt next to the body of his brother. Tom Custer, winner of two Medals of Honor, but who had always been in his brother's shadow, had failed to survive. Rage burned through the general. He had watched as most of five companies had been slaughtered. He knew that another brother Boston was already dead and that his young nephew Henry Reed was gone too. Now Tom.

Custer stood, screamed like a man possessed, and fired his pistol into the air. For an instant the Indians nearest him shrank back, frightened by the sudden insanity. One of them ran forward and Custer killed him with a shot to the forehead. The Sioux flipped back, falling.

Yates shouted, "General, we have to get out now."

"No!" said Custer. "We die here."

The adjutant, Cooke, said, "General, we can break out to the north."

"We sweep the savages from the field and then burn their village."

Yates wiped his mouth with the back of his hand. He turned and looked at the scene around him. The majority of the five companies were dead, the bodies scattered across the slope. The horses killed had formed breastworks with soldiers lying dead behind them. Smoke obscured much of the battlefield. The heat pressed in.

"General, we can break out to the north."

"No," said Custer again. And then he fell back. He struggled to sit up. Blood stained his buckskin jacket.

Yates spun and saw only a couple of officers left alive. Three sergeants were firing, crouched back to back in a triangle, trying to protect one another as the Indians tried to kill them.

The bugler was lying near the general's guidon, dead. Next to him was the regimental sergeant major, also dead. With the general badly wounded, Yates assumed command. He was the senior surviving officer.

"Get to the men and tell them it is time to get out. No orders. Just get out as best you can. It's each man for himself."

A lieutenant looked at the wounded general.

Yates nodded and said, "We can't save the wounded. Every man for himself."

"Yes, sir."

The lieutenant turned and took an arrow in the stomach. The arrowhead pushed through his abdomen and protruded from his back. "Shit" was all he said as he dropped.

Cooke was hit next. He fell to his side, kicked a foot, and died. Yates knelt then, his pistol in his hand, and fired at the Sioux who no longer tried to hide. The fighting was now down to groups of men, two or three or even individuals. The Sioux were darting in with coup sticks, touching the soldiers before fleeing to cover.

Custer was up on his hands and knees, his head down. Blood was pouring from his mouth. In his hand he held his pistol but no longer had the strength to raise and fire it. He seemed to be staring at the body of his brother.

The three sergeants lived as long as they could. They fired in turn, reloading as one of the others covered. But then one of them was hit. He pitched forward, falling on his weapon. As he died, a group of Sioux rushed the other two. They stood to meet the threat.

One of them clubbed an Indian with the barrel of his weapon, bending it. The Sioux fell to the side. As he did, a second one leaped forward and stabbed with a knife. The sergeant took it in the chest. He fell back and as he did, he pulled the trigger of his weapon. It exploded in his hands. He screamed once and then was silent.

The last sergeant threw his rifle at the closest savage. He drew his pistol, shot a warrior through the chest, hit a second, and then turned the pistol on himself. Without giving the Sioux a chance to capture him, he pulled the trigger, blowing his brains out of his head.

The warriors who witnessed the act fell back, away from the dead sergeant. Suicide was an act they didn't understand. It showed strong medicine and they feared the man now, even though he was dead.

Firing from the field was tapering. The soldiers were dying rapidly as the Indians mopped up the resistance. Yates knew there was no chance for escape now. He crouched, firing until his pistol was empty. Tossing it aside, he grabbed the carbine of a dead trooper as the Sioux swarmed over the field.

One of them shot a trooper who lay in a fetal position. Another grabbed the hair of a trooper, trying to scalp him, but the man began to scream. The Indian shot him, killing him, and then finished taking the scalp.

There were only a couple of men left now. Yates knew it was over and there was no way that he could escape. That thought washed over him like the waves on a beach. He was one of the few men left alive and he was about to die. It could be easy, a quick bullet, or hard, with the Sioux dancing around him, laughing at him as he died. No way out.

Still, he couldn't put the gun to his head and pull the trigger. He didn't have the courage. He would make the enemy kill him. He wouldn't give up.

The Indians were racing around now, with little coordination to the attack. They were gaining personal glory as the Seventh died. So few of the cavalrymen were left that they were no longer a threat to the Indians. They were now playing with the few survivors, much as a cat would play with a trapped mouse, trying to make the game last a little longer.

Several of the warriors rushed Yates. He swung his rifle, hitting one man in the head. The force of the blow broke the weapon. Yates threw it away and punched at another Sioux, driving the brave to the ground. He kicked a third and was suddenly feeling good, making a fight out of it. There was a pain in his back and then the sky turned black. Yates fell forward and died.

Now the only members of the Seventh left alive were those who had been wounded. Most were unconscious, unaware of what was happening. Custer was among them, but he still knelt on his hands and knees. Blood dribbled down his chin, dropping to the crimsoned prairie.

A warrior ran toward him, yanked the pistol from his hand, and fired at his temple. The general collapsed, rolling to his back. He was dead before he hit the ground.

For a moment an appalling quiet fell over the field.

Suddenly there was no more shooting, no more shouting, just the quiet moaning from the few wounded. Smoke and dust hung heavy, the acrid stench drifting on the breeze.

From the village, the squaws came, moving among the dead, stripping them and smashing the skulls of the injured. They came to a wounded officer and as they moved in, he sat up suddenly with a loud groan. In his hand, he held a pistol, but he was unable to aim it.

The squaws ran from the strong medicine—a warrior returning from the land beyond. But a Sioux walked up, took the weapon from the soldier, and then killed him. When he was dead, the squaws stole his clothes and slashed his body.

Then, from far to the east, came the sounds of more firing. Other soldiers still lived and the warriors ran from the field of death. They wanted to be in on the kill when the rest of the Seventh Cavalry was eliminated.

THIRTY-FOUR

Firing from the bluff had tapered until it was sporadic. Indian snipers took potshots, rarely hitting anything. It was almost as if they were shooting only to let the soldiers trapped with Reno know they were still out there. In the distance, they could hear heavy firing and assumed that Custer was fighting the Sioux, but no one had any real answers.

The question that had been asked all afternoon still echoed across the bluff. "Where is Custer?"

Kent, lying in a shallow depression, the sun baking his back as he studied the village, knew the answer. Custer and his five companies were dead. His question was, "Where is Brown?"

Benteen had arrived and Reno had stopped him. He stood on the ground, looking up at Benteen who sat on his horse. "You've got to stay here. Half my men are killed."

"My orders are to find Custer."

Both officers could hear the heavy firing filtering down the valley. In the distance, both thought they could see clouds of smoke and dust swirling, but neither man was sure.

"You have to stay," said Reno.

"Mount your command and we'll ride to relieve."

"No. I've wounded. I can't leave them here." Reno looked as if he was going to break down.

Thomas Weir listened to the argument for a few moments and then told one of his lieutenants, "Mount the men. We're pressing on."

Weir's company left the hilltop riding to the west. A moment later they were joined by Benteen and three more companies. As they worked their way to the west, the sounds of the firing tapered slowly, becoming single shots.

As they reached a high point, the Sioux came boiling out of the ravines. Weir's men fired quickly and stopped the Indian attack, but they were joined by a thousand other. Weir had no choice but to retreat.

Kent, along with the men who had remained behind with Reno, watched as the soldiers returned. It was a running gunfight, though the Indians were pressing them hard. They reached the top of the bluff and spread out, falling in with Reno's men as Benteen worked to erect a defense.

"What happened?" demanded Reno.

Benteen refused to answer. But other men were talking.

"Savages all over."

"Thousands of them."

"Came right at us screaming and shooting and not afraid of a thing."

Munday leaned close to Kent. "What's happened?"

Kent looked at his watch. It was nearly five in the afternoon. That meant that Custer had already had his fight. Most historians claimed the final battle lasted no more than an hour, probably about forty minutes.

Quietly, so that no one else could hear, he said, "Custer is dead."

"What about Brown and the others?"

"I don't know," snapped Kent. He was suddenly angry with her and almost said something about asking stupid questions. But he knew the question wasn't stupid. It was one that had to be asked, and he was mad because he had no answer for it. He thought that he knew, was afraid that he knew. Brown had played it too close and got caught in the battle.

He took a deep breath and looked at her. "Can you recover your camera?"

"Brown had the equipment. He has to recover it."

"Great," said Kent.

"We can punch out of here," said Munday. "We can then come back later."

"Or we can wait."

"Why?" she asked, her voice high.

Kent wiped the sweat from his face. The answer was

obvious. Brown would wait to make sure that all his men were back. He would not leave the field until he was sure that everyone was accounted for. He wouldn't assume anything. He'd wait to be sure, especially since there was no immediate danger.

"We wait," he said, "because it's the right thing to do."

Munday fell silent for a moment and then asked, "Is this like that boy you saved?"

"What?"

"You refuse to understand the situation. You act because you think something is right."

"I'm staying because Brown would stay."

Firing erupted then. A dozen weapons and a few arrows. Two soldiers shouted. More firing and then silence.

"We stay here," said Munday, "we could get killed."

"I won't leave my friends."

"Look," she said, "this isn't a one way trip. We can get out, and then come back an hour from now, or two, or tomorrow morning. We don't have to expose ourselves to the enemy firing anymore."

"Men are straggling in," said Kent. "By tomorrow, twenty-four men from F Company who should have been killed but who somehow avoided riding into the massacre will arrive here." He began talking faster then, to keep Munday from interrupting. "And men from the valley below us, men who everyone thought were dead, will make their way up here."

"But why wait?" asked Munday.

Now Kent was silent. He listened to the firing drifting to them from the Custer battlefield. Single shots as the Indians eliminated the wounded, or just shot at the bodies of the dead. He listened to the moaning of the wounded, their calls for help or water or relief from their pain. He listened to the cries of the pack animals and the frightened horses. And he listened to the Indians shouting to each other, a sound that faded as drums began in the village. The celebration of their victory over the soldiers.

"We have to get out of here."

"You want the others to see us suddenly disappear?

Every one of these men is going to be interviewed for life. The least little thing is going to be analyzed from every angle."

"We can hide among the pack animals. No one will see us. They're all looking out, toward the Indian village."

Kent was tired of the argument. He turned and stared down into the valley below them. In the distance he could see the warriors moving, running, dancing around. There was firing in the village and some of the soldiers believed that it was Custer carrying out the attack. Kent knew better. It was the Indians celebrating their victory. The shooting was sporadic, single shots. Not the heavy firing of a full blown cavalry charge.

Bullets whined around them. Periodic shots by snipers who climbed from the river or tried to circle around the rear of the bluff to kill another soldier and to gain more glory. But that was more harassment than anything else. The majority of the Sioux and the Cheyenne were in the camp, telling everyone who would listen about their exploits and their personal bravery.

Munday dropped her face to the ground and covered her head. She didn't move for a few moments.

"We have to wait," said Kent. He wanted to explain it further but knew that she would refuse to understand.

The night was more of the same. The soldiers worked to dig their firing pits deeper, using their canteen cups, mess kits and knives to scrape at the sun-hardened earth. They pushed boxes from the pack train forward, stacked equipment in front of them, and tried to hide on the exposed plateau. Indian snipers kept up a steady firing, using captured cavalry rifles against the defenders.

And all through the night, there were drums in the village. Fires burned brightly as if the Sioux and Cheyenne feared nothing. They were celebrating something. The soldiers with Reno and Benteen couldn't understand it, refusing to believe that anything could have happened to Custer. They figured he was defending ground just as they were.

On the center of the plateau, surrounded by the pack animals and the horses, lay the wounded. The thought was that the animals would provide some protection.

Kent watched it all. He kept his rifle pointed down, at the Indian village, but he didn't fire. Suddenly he was afraid of making an inadvertent change. Killing one of the Indians might set up a ripple that would echo forward. He tried not to think about it being too late already.

As the night progressed, the celebrating in the village became louder and the fires burned brighter but the firing around them tapered until it was only an occasional shot from one of the few lingering Indians. The siege was ending already.

"How about now?" asked Munday, finally. "Your friends have had plenty of time to get up here."

"No," said Kent. "We stay."

"Then I'm leaving. You'll have to remain here by yourself."

"No," he said again. "You can't do that."

"Look," she said, her voice rising. "Look, we can get out and come back later. Tomorrow afternoon. The next day. We don't have to stay here."

There was a quiet moaning to the rear. One of the wounded asking for water, asking for help, pleading with God to make the pain go away. There was a scream then as one of the men was suddenly doubled in pain. A piercing scream that sounded almost like a war whoop of an attacking savage.

"I can't stand it," snapped Munday. "I have to get out."

"Things are improving," said Kent. "The Sioux are slipping away. Patience."

The firing woke him. A wild burst of it down the bluffs, from the direction of the river. Kent rolled around and watched as a squad of men, loaded down with canteens, ran for the safety of the bluff. The Indians were chasing them, whooping and hollering and firing at them. Soldiers on the bluff shot back, providing a covering fire. Volley after volley poured down the slope until the soldiers reached safety. They rolled over the top of the bluff, out of the line of firing, lying there among the canteens and equipment, trying to catch their breaths.

Other soldiers scrambled forward to grab at the water. Benteen, standing erect as if afraid of nothing, yelled, "The wounded first. Water to the wounded first."

A few men picked up the canteens and took them to the center of the bluff and began giving the wounded the water. The moaning quieted as some of the men, once their thirst was quenched, fell into a fitful sleep.

"How much longer?" asked Munday. "How much longer are you going to stay here?"

"Until I know what happened to my friends."

THIRTY-FIVE

There was no attempt to storm the plateau the next day. Indians moved around the base of the bluff, fired up at the soldiers and once they seemed to be forming for an attack, but heavy firing drove them from the field. They scattered, returned the fire halfheartedly, apparently abandoning the idea of attacking the soldiers.

All through the day the men were asking each other, "Where is Custer? Why isn't he here?"

Munday had given up demanding that they return to the future. Kent's answer was always the same. He wanted to wait until Brown, Thompson, and Baily had a chance to get to them. He wouldn't abandon his friends.

"They're dead," said Munday in exasperation.

"You can't know that."

She glanced around and lowered her voice. "Everyone with Custer is dead. You know it and I know it."

Kent didn't say anything about that. Instead, he said, "We'll wait." Glancing up at the sun, now high overhead, he added, "The Indians are going to be getting out soon. Then we'll be safe."

"No reason to stay here," she said.

"No reason not to," Kent responded.

There was sudden activity in the Indian camp about mid-afternoon. The men on the bluffs, using the binoculars, couldn't tell what was happening. All they knew was that the Indians had given up shooting at them. They had abandoned their firing positions. They stopped their sniping, and they disappeared into the distance.

More rumors swept the bluff. "Custer is coming."

"The general beat them."

"Custer finally has broken through."

But there was never the firing that would suggest another attack by Custer and there wasn't the cloud of dust that his column would have raised. The men waited, afraid to leave their positions on the bluff, each of them wondering where the rest of the regiment was. They wondered why the general hadn't ridden to their rescue as they expected.

Benteen moved toward Reno who sat with his back to a box, staring at the ground between his feet. Benteen said, "I want to take a scouting party out."

"No," said Reno. "We stay here. We can't divide the regiment again."

"We've got to recon. We have to learn what is happening."

"No," said Reno. "Everyone stays right here until Custer arrives. Then you'll have your answer."

Benteen looked as if he was going to say more, but then realized that half the soldiers there were listening to the exchange. Anything he said would soon spread through the remainder of the regiment. Instead, he spun and walked away, ignoring Reno's demands that he return to discuss it.

Kent rolled to his back and stared up into the bright blue of the Montana sky. There were birds overhead. From below came the quiet sounds of the river. With the firing ended and the drumming of the Sioux and Cheyenne finished, it was peaceful on the bluff. A hot, lazy, summer day; the biggest worry now a bad sunburn.

"Now?" asked Munday sounding like a broken record. "Can we get out now?"

Kent sat up and shaded his eyes with one hand. "You could get out by yourself."

She shrugged and stared at him. "We're in this together."

"Then you understand my feelings."

"No really. We get home and then come back, targeting it twenty-four or forty-eight hours later."

"But what if Brown and Thompson show up during that time. They'll think we abandoned them."

"That doesn't make sense," said Munday.

Kent shrugged and said, "It's how I feel. Besides, the

danger is now over. The Indians are getting out."

Munday turned to look down into the valley. She could make out some activity there, but couldn't tell what they were doing. She sat back. "So we stay."

"No reason to get out now," said Kent.

The night was quiet. The Indians were gone and another expedition down to the river met with no resistance. They filled all the canteens and made it back to the top of the bluff with no shots being fired.

All through the night, the exhausted soldiers listened for sounds of the Indians or noise from the regiment. They still asked where Custer was, some of them assuming that the general was chasing the Indians who had now disappeared. They waited, fearing the worst, that somehow the general and his men had been killed. Most of them figured that Custer and the majority of his battalion would be holed up much as they were.

Dawn broke bright. With binoculars, the officers could tell that the Indian camp was gone. There was smoke in the distance where the Indians had set the prairie on fire to cover their line of march. Reno, now convinced that the danger was past, dispatched scouts to locate Custer and the men with him.

The rest of the command stayed on the hilltop waiting for word about Custer. They watched the horizon to the west and at last saw a cloud of dust rising above a column that moved toward them. The men began to cheer, sure that this was Custer, now returning to gather the rest of his regiment.

The men stood, cheering, waving their hats or their hands, motioning the column closer. And as it came closer, the cheering slowly died and the waving stopped. The men could recognize none of the soldiers and it was obvious that it wasn't Custer and the other five companies of the Seventh.

Two soldiers broke from the column and rushed forward. These were the scouts that Reno had sent out earlier. One of them rode straight at the major, reined in his horse and slid from the saddle. Without saluting, he said, "Custer's dead. Everyone with him is dead."

Word spread through the camp on the hilltop rapidly, each man repeating the words as if it would somehow make the news untrue. "The general's dead. All of them are dead."

Munday touched Kent on the shoulder and said, "Satisfied?"

He whirled on her, his eyes blazing, his face a mask of hatred. "Not until I see for myself. Not until then."

While the surgeon moved among the wounded, trying to help them, a party was organized to ride the four miles to the west. Kent volunteered to go with them. Munday stood there dumbfounded.

"Why?" she demanded.

"To retrieve our equipment," he said. But the real reason was that he wanted to be sure that Brown, Thompson, and Baily had been killed in the fight. He wanted to give them every opportunity to reappear.

Munday shrugged and mounted a horse. After two days, she knew that there would be no stopping Kent now. He wanted to see the battlefield.

With fifty others, they rode out, to the west, passing the point that Captain Weir had reached on the afternoon of the twenty-fifth. They could catch glimpses of the hillside where Custer and his command died. They could see the white objects that were the naked bodies of the dead.

A silence descended the column as they rode on. Finally they came up, out of a small ravine and to the top of the hill. Spread out below them were the bodies of Custer and his men. Nearly two hundred of them, scattered on the slope.

"Jesus," said Kent.

The column halted and Kent slid from the saddle. He stood there feeling sick to his stomach. To his right was the sound of flies buzzing strongly. He turned and looked at the mutilated face of a dead soldier. His head was misshapen from the blows of Sioux war clubs. The fingers of one hand were missing and there were deep cuts on his legs, belly and back.

"Jesus," he said again. He crouched down and stared at the ground by his feet.

"You seen enough?" asked Munday.

Kent stood up and looked at her. "I have to find their bodies."

Munday nodded. "I'm staying here." She turned and faced to the north, away from the battlefield.

Kent turned and began walking down the slope, moving toward the west where there was a cluster of bodies where Custer and the regiment had died. He had to be careful because there were parts of bodies scattered everywhere. The air was filled with the stench of the dead.

Sickened, he moved among the bodies, looking at them. Some were so disfigured that no one could recognize them. Tom Custer was identified by a tattoo on his arm. It was the only thing about him that anyone could recognize.

Kent saw Custer's body lying on the ground, a bullet hole in the left side. Blood stained the skin and the ground under him. Kent looked away, not wanting to see any more.

But there was so much more to see. More dead men, their bodies ripped apart. Pieces of bodies. Arms and legs and hands and feet. Fingers were scattered on the ground. There were internal organs and brains and broken bodies.

And then Kent saw the remains of Brown. Like the others he had been mutilated. His eyes had been gouged out and there were cuts in the thighs, belly, and arms. Kent crouched there, looked at the dead man and wanted to ask what had happened, but the answer was obvious. Brown had stayed with Custer to the very end.

Close to him was Pete Baily, dead and mutilated. Kent looked down and shook his head. There was no sign of Thompson, but Kent knew that she was dead too. There was no sense searching for her among the dead. It was one sight that he didn't want to see. He'd already seen too much.

Slowly he walked up the slope to where Munday

waited. He spoke softly when he reached her. "They're dead."

She turned and looked. "Our equipment?"

"I don't know where it is. I don't know where Brown's horse is. Everything is gone. Stolen by the Sioux."

"Can we get out now?"

Kent nodded. "Yeah. As soon as we can separate ourselves from the soldiers, we'll get out."

THIRTY-SIX

Jackson met them in the conference room outside the control point. He pointed at a chair and once both Munday and Kent were seated, Jackson said, "Your friends have gone home."

Kent, fresh from the battlefield of the Little Bighorn, didn't understand. He thought Jackson was referring to Brown, Thompson, and Baily. All he could say was, "What?"

Jackson explained, "Those left behind had opted to go home. Return to their own times. That option is now open to you."

"Wait," he said. "I have to return to 1876 and retrieve Brown, Thompson, and Baily."

"They're dead," said Jackson.

"How do you know?" asked Kent. He'd said nothing about it since retrieval.

"We keep careful records here."

"Well, it doesn't matter," said Kent. "I'll just hit the field before they get killed. We'll get them out."

"I'm afraid that our operation has been shut down. There will be no more forays into the past."

"I don't understand."

Jackson stood up and paced in front of the table. He walked to the wall, turned, walked back, and finally stopped. He gripped the back of the chair and said, "Our research tells me that we are back on the right path. Or very close to it with only a few, trivial variations. History is in good shape . . ."

"We have an obligation to get those people back."

"Can't be done," said Jackson. "We aren't going to take a chance on screwing things up again."

"We have an obligation to those people," Kent shouted.

"We have a bigger obligation to the world. We have no right to meddle in history, changing it to suit our purposes. No, it's all over."

Munday felt the color drain from her face. There were a hundred questions that she wanted to ask but didn't know where to start. Instead, she sat mute, looking from Kent to Jackson and back again.

"My friends . . ."

"Gave their lives in a cause they believed in. It was Brown who demanded that we change the past."

"To put it back," said Kent.

"Whatever," said Jackson. "The point is that we are not going to travel in time again. With one exception. You can return to your time, if you want."

"NO!" screamed Munday.

Both men looked at her. She shook her head and then said to Kent, "You can't return to your own time."

"What's going on here," said Jackson.

Kent broke in. "We can worry about that later."

Jackson grinned. "This discussion is over. There will be no return to 1876. History is as it stands at this moment."

"But . . ."

"The orders are given," said Jackson. "And I'm not going to stand here and listen to your arguments. There is nothing that I can do and there is nothing you can do. Accept it."

Kent turned to face the man but he was walking toward the door. He stopped and said, "When you have made your decision about your future, I'll be in my office." He left the room then.

Kent leaned forward, his head in his hands. "What the hell good is time travel if you don't use it."

"To change time?" asked Munday gently.

"To help your friends."

She reached out to touch him but let her hand drop to the table top. "Where do you stop?"

"What?"

"Where do you stop? You want to make a little change so that your friends don't die at the Little Bighorn. So a father wants a little change so that his daughter doesn't drown. Or a husband wants to bring some medicine back from the future to save his wife. How do you decide?"

"The difference is that my friends weren't supposed to die at the Little Bighorn."

"But they did. Maybe it's best to leave everything as it is. Don't mess with the time line now that it's stabilized."

"They deserve some help. It's not fair."

"Listen to yourself," said Munday. "It's not fair? Nothing about life is fair. That's just the way it is."

Kent fell back in his chair, his mind racing. The human race had yet to invent something that it didn't use. The best intentions often got overlooked in political struggles. Men and women who were ambitious often used everything to further those ambitions. Someday, someone would reassemble the time travel project. He was sure of it. In fact, he had access to another machine if he wanted to use it. The Tucker Transfer still existed in the past and Jackson had promised him a trip to that time if he wanted it. If he decided to return home.

Munday broke in on his thoughts. "What are you thinking about?"

"What to do?"

"I have a suggestion," said Munday quietly.

"What?"

"Stay here with me. I want you to stay."

"You sure?"

"Yes. Please."

Kent looked at her and thought about what they had been through together. He thought about Gettysburg and then the Little Bighorn, and time traveling and the fact that he had nothing to go back to. Friends in Texas with T. R. B. Tucker, but no family and no wife. No one really waiting for him. Just the machine Tucker had built.

"Okay," he said.

"You mean it?"

"Yeah," he said, his voice firmer. "I mean it."